BY RICHARD J. LOWE

Shieldmaiden Tales
Fire in the North
Clans of the Silver Hills
Beyond the Sunset Isles
Feybane

Science Fiction
Box

RICHARD J. LOWE

Fire in the North

First published in paperback by Richard J Lowe in 2017

http://www.facebook.com/richardjloweauthor/

Cover illustration by Sarah Mercer
http://Sarah-mercer.co.uk/

for Amanda

CHAPTER 1

After Lord Denly died, the Kingdom of Asterland was in turmoil. It wasn't his actual death, which was due to nothing more sinister than old age, but subsequent events that caused the turmoil. King Stephen decreed that all Lord Denly's lands were to go to Lord Mayhew, the King's cousin, proving that nepotism was alive and well in his kingdom. Unfortunately, Lord Mayhew was a southern lord, and Lord Denly's lands were in the north of the country. Many Northerners resented Lord Mayhew's appointment for the obvious geographical reason that they disliked anyone south of the river Treal. Lord Denly's son, Simon, resented it for a more personal reason - he felt he should have inherited his father's estate. This resentment would not take much to turn into open insurrection.

Further north, past the borders of troubled Asterland, beyond the bleak Troll Fells lay the Silver Hills. The dwarven clans of the Silver Hills did not, as a rule, become involved in events that occurred in the south. They were kept busy with occasional inter-clan squabbles and constant warring with the savage goblin tribes of the north. This isolationist policy was about to change.

This is the story of two individuals who would have a

1

vital role to play in the future of both the Kingdom of Asterland and the dwarven clans of the Silver Hills. In an Astish town called Stonebridge, situated on the northern border with the Troll Fells, a somewhat clichéd meeting in a drinking establishment begins our tale...

John cursed the persistent drizzle that seemed to seep through every seam of his clothing. He had been walking all day and was cold, wet and tired. John pulled his rain cloak closer about him and continued to trudge along the muddy road into town. After crossing the stone bridge which gave the town its name, he saw a painted inn sign depicting a happy-looking pig, which promised a meal, a beer and a warm bed. This prompted him to change course, crossing the road and entering the timber-clad two storey building. He was grateful to see a crackling fire warming the large, busy common room. The room was filled with the sound of conversation, drifting clouds of pipe smoke and the twanging of a stringed instrument being strummed by a distinctly amateur troubadour. John found the only unoccupied table, dropped his pack on the floor and himself on a chair. His clothes slowly shed their load of water, which formed a small puddle on the wooden floor.

As he was wringing the water out of his cloak, he heard the door open behind him and felt a cold, damp blast of air. He half turned in his seat and saw a short, stocky woman standing in the doorway. She had cropped dark hair, was dressed in scale armour made of overlapping metal plates, wore a sword at her hip and a shield on her back. She was a dwarf of the clans of the Silver Hills if he wasn't mistaken.

Scowling, she surveyed the inn and then marched to the only empty seat available, the other chair at John's table. 'This seat is now taken,' she stated and sat down with a clank.

'Uh, hello,' he greeted her.

She did not reply as she removed the shield from her back and rested it against the table leg.

'What's a dwarf doing so far south?' John persisted, trying to get a conversation started.

'None of your business pal,' she said. She beckoned the waitress over and curtly ordered an ale.

'I'll have one too,' said John cheerfully. Then, having spotted the scowl on the dwarf's face, he said, 'I'll pay,' and passed a few coins to the waitress.

That seemed to instantly improve the dwarf's mood, a broad smile breaking out on her rugged, but not unattractive face.

'The name's Bienia Ironfist,' she said, thrusting out a sword-calloused hand.

'John Cotterill,' he said, wincing a little as his hand was all but crushed in a fierce handshake.

'So, John, what do you do? You don't look like a farmer,' she said, glancing at his battered leather armour and sword.

'My old dad was a farmer, my brothers are farmers, but I broke with family tradition. I'm a bounty hunter. You?'

'Shieldmaiden.' She tapped her shield.

They sat in silence for a few moments until the waitress returned and deposited two frothing tankards of ale on the table.

'Best keep them coming,' said Bienia as she lifted her

tankard and swiftly drained it. 'Ah, that's better.' She smacked her lips in appreciation. 'Another!'

He sat and watched in amazement as a second ale followed the first. This seemed to satisfy her thirst, and the third tankard stayed on the table as she turned to John and asked 'Much gold in bounty hunting?'

A shadow fell over the table as their conversation was rudely interrupted.

'What's a bloody dwarf doing in here?' The speaker was a big belligerent man who was, by the looks of it, quite drunk.

Bienia looked up coolly and said 'Having a drink. Problem?'

'Damn right there's a problem. I don't like dwarves.'

'Hey, just back off. We don't want any trouble,' said John.

The man turned his glassy gaze John's way. 'Stay out of it. This is between me and the runt.'

John stood up and unsheathed the top inch of his sword. 'Think again.'

The man looked unsteadily at John and his sword before the waitress came and took him by his arm. 'Come on Trevor, no need for this. Why don't you come have another drink?'

'A drink?' asked Trevor stupidly.

'I'll buy him one,' said John.

'No need love, he's still got one on the bar,' said the waitress. She then gently led the big man away to retrieve his drink.

John sat down heavily. 'Well, that was exciting.'

'Thanks, but I could have handled him myself,' said Bienia.

'I was starting to wonder what I'd done,' said John.

'He's drunk; he would have been a pushover. So, back to my question. Is there much gold in bounty hunting?'

'Some. Pays better than shit shovelling and I'm my own boss.'

Bienia snorted a short laugh. 'Maybe I should try my hand at it. Soldiering may be steady pay, but taking orders from some of the arses I've served under.' She shook her head, took a long drink of ale and then said, 'Arses' again for emphasis.

'So, you're not soldiering anymore?'

'I'm currently seeking new opportunities, thanks for asking.'

He thought back to his last job. He'd nearly been skewered by the second sheep rustler while the first kept him talking. Bounty hunting had been getting more dangerous lately; people seemed more desperate.

'Maybe. You know, I could use a partner to watch my back. Who would get a fair share of the bounty, of course.'

'You ask me just like that? What makes you think you can trust me?' asked Bienia, clearly taken aback by his forthright proposal.

'Dwarves are honest and honourable aren't they?' He was sure he'd heard that somewhere.

'Hah, honest as the day is long. Honourable? Not so much.' A wry grin came with that statement.

'So, be honest with me,' said John.

Bienia considered this, drumming her fingers on the table. After a moment, her deliberations completed, she said, 'You can rely on me to watch your back.' She then spat in her right hand, held it out and said, 'My sword and shield for your cause.'

John spat in his palm and endured the bone-crunching handshake for a second time. With that formality out of the way he raised his tankard, 'To a profitable partnership.'

'I'll drink to that, let's make some gold,' said Biena.

With this new partnership forged, the two of them passed the evening with ale and swapped stories, both truthful and tall, of their exploits.

*   *   *

John lurched down the stairs into the inn's common room. He was a little hungover, and his stomach churned over when he caught sight of Bienia tucking into a hearty breakfast of bread, cheese and sausage. 'Morning John,' she said waving cheerfully. 'Come have some breakfast.'

John paled, 'I think I'll pass, thanks'

'Your loss,' she said with a shrug.

'I'm going to head out and find us some work.' He stopped at the door. 'We did agree to be partners last night, right?'

'Yes we did.' Bienia had impaled a sausage with her knife and waved it around for emphasis. 'And I, for one, am looking forward to a lucrative future.' She took a big bite out of the sausage and chewed, a satisfied look on her face.

John opened the door, wincing at the full sunlight that hit his face as he stepped outside. Typical, he thought, the weather clears up as soon as he's not on the road.

The morning was full of the sounds of market traders setting up their stalls, most of which were being laid out with produce from the surrounding farms. John threaded his way through the marketplace until he found what he was looking for, a long low building with a crown and shield painted on the wall identifying it as the local watch house. Partially obscuring the painted emblem was a stall selling leather goods.

'Belt sir? Keep your trousers up, guaranteed,' the trader offered, sweeping his hand across his neatly laid out stock. John steadfastly ignored the man and entered the open, unattended door.

'Hello? Anyone here?' he called out as he entered a large room that contained several tatty looking desks.

He spotted a noticeboard on one wall and headed over to see if there were any wanted posters. He was disappointed to find only an out of date patrol rota and a faded poster advertising a second-hand horse drawn cart for sale.

'Can I help you?' a smooth male voice said from behind him.

John turned to see a tall, dark-haired, handsome man wearing a smart blue tunic. He noted the watch captain's silver badge with its crown and shield insignia pinned to the man's chest.

'Uh, yes, I was looking for your wanted posters,' said John. He then added, 'I'm a bounty hunter,' by way of explanation.

'We can handle our own warrants, we have no need for contract workers,' the man said dismissively.

'There's nothing at all? No job too small, no job too tough.'

'There may be something.' The man looked thoughtful. 'I've not seen you before; you're new in town aren't you?'

'Yes, I am. The name's John Cotterill.'

7

'I am Captain Lucien Marrian.' He managed to make his name sound capitalised.

'You said there is some work for me?' John asked.

'Yes, I may have something for you. A small matter, non-payment of taxes. I have a warrant for the arrest of a Benjamin Threetwottle.'

While Captain Marrian was talking, he had walked over to one of the desks and was leafing through a messy stack of paper.

'Ah hah, here it is,' he said as he pulled a sheet of paper from near the bottom of the pile.

Captain Marrian handed the warrant to John.

'He'll probably give you some sob story about his poor sick children or some such. Pay it no heed and bring him here.'

John checked the address. 'Wheat Lane, where is that? I'm afraid I don't know my way around.'

'By the Gods man, use some bloody initiative. I'm not paying you so I can stand here giving you instructions all day.'

'Sorry,' John reflexively apologised.

'Well? What are you waiting for?'

'The pay. How much exactly?'

'For this piffling job? I'm in a generous mood, six shillings.'

'Thank you, most kind.'

It was galling for John, to be polite to this man, but in his experience, it was best to stay on the right side of the local law enforcement. Plus he was going to get paid, even if it wasn't particularly 'generous' in his opinion.

'Go on then. Go get your man.'

John took this cue to leave, returning to the Contented

Pig Inn. Once there, a quick conversation with the innkeeper got him the directions to Wheat Lane. Within half an hour, John and Bienia were standing outside of a ramshackle wooden hut on the poorer side of town.

'My first bounty hunting job already,' said Bienia, sounding pleased.

'Don't get too carried away. This isn't really a tough assignment,' said John as he knocked on the door.

They waited for a few seconds before the door was pulled open a crack.

'Benjamin Threetwottle?' asked John.

'Yes, who are you?'

John replied by wedging his boot in the open doorway.

'Hey, stop that!' Benjamin tried to push the door shut.

Bienia put a stop to that by dropping her shoulder and charging into the door. It gave way with a splintering crack. The man behind it was flung backwards and he, the broken door and Bienia crashed to the floor in an untidy stack.

John peered through the now open doorway at the dwarf, who was lying on top of the door which, in turn, was on top of Benjamin.

'Is he…?' he tailed off.

'Dead? No. Unconscious? Yes, I think so,' said Bienia as she clambered to her feet. 'Do we need to tell him he's under arrest or something?'

'I don't think we need to bother,' said John. He helped her lift the door from on top of the prone figure.

Bienia stood looking down at their unconscious prisoner, her hands on her hips. 'So, how do we get him back to the watch house?'

'Stay here. I'll find us some transport.'

John stepped out of the broken doorway and had a look

up and down the lane. A cart laden with cabbages was rumbling past. Stepping into the road, he waved his hands above his head, prompting the driver to reign in the ancient looking horse, bringing the cart to a stop.

'What d'ya want?' the driver asked.

'Are you headed for the market?'

'No, I'm takin' me cabbages for a tour o' the town.' This reply was delivered dead-pan.

John smiled thinly. 'Can we get a ride?'

'We?'

It was then that Bienia appeared, her arms under Benjamin Threetwottle's armpits, dragging him out of the hut.

'We have a prisoner to deliver to the watch house,' said John.

The driver looked at Bienia, the man she was dragging, John and finally John's sword. 'Reckon it cost ya,' he said.

They settled on two pennies, which John paid in advance. The two bounty hunters and the apprehended tax evader then rode in the back with the cabbages to the market square and the watch house.

CHAPTER 2

John and Bienia hauled the still unconscious Benjamin Threetwottle through the open watch house door. The proprietor of the leather goods stall outside wisely refrained from trying to sell them anything, instead making a show of not paying them any attention.

This time, although the door was open, the room beyond was not empty. An overweight man was sitting behind one of the desks, his feet up and a mug cupped in his hands. His tunic had a cloth badge depicting a crown and shield sewn onto it, identifying him as a member of the watch. He looked up at the pair who were awkwardly holding the unconscious prisoner between them. Their height difference did not make it easy.

'Drunk?' he asked.

'Prisoner. Threetwottle. Got a warrant for his arrest.' John held out the warrant with his free hand.

The watchman sighed, reluctantly put his mug down, got to his feet and ambled over to retrieve the proffered warrant. He gave the page a cursory inspection and pointed to an empty chair.

While they dumped their prisoner on the chair, the man

scribbled something on the warrant and added it to a large pile of paper on his desk. He counted out six silver shillings and handed them to John.

'You're John Cotterill, right?' He did not wait for confirmation. 'Captain's in there, said he wanted a word.' He jerked a thumb over his shoulder indicating a doorway bearing a brass plate with the word 'Captain' engraved on it then returned to his previously held position, behind the desk, sipping his hot beverage, pointedly ignoring them.

John handed Bienia her half of the bounty. 'I'll find out what he wants and meet you back at the Contented Pig.'

Pocketing the coins, she nodded and made her exit.

John knocked on the door to the Captain's office.

'Come!' came the shout from inside.

John opened the door and stepped into the room. The walls were painted in the same whitewash as the main room, and Captain Marrian was sitting behind a standard issue tatty wooden desk. The only concession to personalisation of the office was on the desk – a miniature portrait of a stern-looking woman in her early thirties. Beside this picture was a gently steaming mug of the same beverage that was being enjoyed by the watchman outside the office.

'Ah, Cotterill. Sit.' Captain Marrian pointed at a low chair the other side of his desk.

John complied and found the chair uncomfortable. It also put him in a sitting position lower than Captain Marrian. Probably on purpose he thought.

'Mister Threetwottle. I am right in assuming you have apprehended him?'

'Yes, brought him in just now. No trouble.'

'Did he try giving some pathetic excuse?'

'Yes, but I ignored it.' John wasn't sure why he lied, perhaps he was trying to give Marrian what he wanted to hear.

'Excellent. It seems you are indeed a capable bounty hunter.'

'I like to think so. Like I said, no job too small.'

'Or too large?' asked Marrian.

'Of course,' said John.

'Good, good. I may have some more, important, work for you. Tell me, are you known by any of the townsfolk?'

'No sir, unless you count the bar staff at the Contented Pig.'

'That will be an advantage bringing this particular individual into custody.' Marrian picked up a piece of paper from his desk.

'You know I can handle that,' said John.

'The miscreant in question is guilty of plotting against the crown. She recognises all of my men, they have been unable to catch her. I require you to apprehend her discreetly.'

John's eyebrows raised imperceptibly. A woman giving the town watch the run around? Probably why the pompous fool wanted this kept quiet.

'Discretion would be extra,' said John.

'Of course, of course. A sum of, shall we say, four gold crowns on completion?'

Four crowns was a lot for a simple arrest. John thought the captain sounded desperate and so decided to push for more. 'You might say four, I'd say six.'

'Very well, six it is,' agreed Marrian quickly.

'Right then.' John felt like he maybe hadn't asked for enough.

'This is the miscreant,' said Marrian as he passed the sheet of paper he had been holding to John. On it was a drawing of a woman's face.

'That's it? A drawing, no name?' said John.

'She has many aliases, they're written on the back.'

John flipped the paper over and saw a list of over a dozen names.

'Right then. Six gold crowns to bring in the lady of many names for crimes against the crown,' said John.

'One more thing. She is wanted dead or alive, so no need to be gentle.'

'Fine,' said John, stuffing the picture into a pocket.

'Remember, discretion is required. This needs to be quiet, no brawling on the streets.'

'Discretion is my middle name,' said John, hoping he sounded sincere, before demonstrating his discretion by discreetly leaving.

CHAPTER 3

John and Bienia had their midday meal in the common room of the Contented Pig. The inn was fairly busy; however, the troubadour was absent, and the clientèle were better behaved than the night before.

'So what's the job?' Bienia asked, pushing her now empty plate to one side.

'The watch captain wants us to arrest this woman,' said John, placing the drawing he had been given on the table in front of him.

'What did she do?'

'Apparently, she's some sort of traitor to the crown or something. The captain wasn't big on details.'

Bienia took a sip of ale and then suddenly looked, startled, past John's shoulder.

'Don't look now, but she's behind you.'

John turned to look and saw the woman sitting at a corner table. She was dressed in a body-hugging black tunic and matching, tightly fitting leggings. He couldn't see her carrying any weapons, or anywhere for her to conceal one.

'I said don't look,' said Bienia.

There was a pause while John continued staring.

'She doesn't look very dangerous,' said Bienia.

'I don't know,' said John. 'Dangerously good looking.' He turned back to examine the picture. It really didn't do her justice. He looked at her again, taking in her shoulder length blond hair, blue eyes and great figure.

'Hey,' Bienia said as she waved her hand in front of his face, 'stop thinking with what's in your britches, and start thinking about what we are going to do.'

'Do? Right. What we do next,' said John, 'is we follow her, find out what she's up to.'

'So, we're not just going to go and arrest her now?'

'No, not yet at least. For one thing, it's a bit public. Secondly, I want to find out what sort of plot she's involved in,' said John.

'Do I get a say?' asked Bienia.

'Oh damn. Of course, I'm just used to operating alone. This partner thing is going to take a bit of getting used to.'

'Then my say is' – Bienia paused melodramatically – 'let's follow her and find out what she's up to.'

'Glad that's cleared up,' said John drily. 'We should take turns. I'll go first.'

'Fine, you best get going then.' Bienia nodded towards the far door where the woman was leaving. John waited until the door had closed behind her before he followed her out.

Bienia picked up her tankard, looked at it, and said, 'Looks like it's just you and me again.'

'Although...' Her gaze shifted from her tankard to the door. 'Maybe I should make sure the tall fella doesn't get into any trouble.'

She then downed what was left of her ale, and followed John out of the door.

John tailed the woman as she wandered the marketplace. She stopped briefly to buy a bag of plums and then moved on, browsing the different stalls as she ate one. He worked his way across the market, avoiding eye contact with the traders trying to sell him 'the freshest vegetables in the north of the kingdom', 'two cabbages for the price of one' or 'a thrupenny fish'. The leather goods trader saw him as he walked by his stall and leapt to his feet.

'How about a new pair of boots? Nice and waterproof,' said the trader as he waved the aforementioned footwear about enthusiastically.

'No thanks. I already have some.' John pointed to his feet.

'Ah, but these are rubbed with beeswax and oil to provide maximum protection.'

'Maybe later,' John said, telling a little white lie. Checking on his target, he saw her disappear down a side street. Hastily, he followed, cursing as he saw he had lost sight of her.

He had just started to jog down the side street when he was tripped by a black booted foot and went sprawling into the dirt. John was impressed. He had totally missed her lurking in the shadows of the building. He was, however, finding it hard to share his admiration with her as his air supply was being curtailed by the choke hold he was in.

'You're following me. Why?' she asked curtly.

John let out a low gurgle in reply.

'What? Oh.' She re-arranged her grip so that it wasn't life threatening. 'You're following me. Why?'

'Coincidence?' offered John.

'Wrong, try again,' she said calmly. 'Are you working for that traitorous dog, Lucien?'

'Who?' asked John, feigning ignorance.

'Tall, handsome, arrogant. Captain of the watch. I saw you go to see him.'

'Ah. Right. Look, I'm just a contractor.'

'That's more like it. Now, I'm going to ask you again. Why were you following me?'

'I'm starting to wonder that myself,' quipped John.

She banged the side of his face into the ground. 'Just answer the damned question.'

'Ow, that hurt,' John complained, earning another head ringing collision with the street.

'Alright, alright. I'm a bounty hunter.'

'A bounty hunter? He wants to arrest me?' she sounded incredulous, 'That's bold even for Lucien.'

'You're a wanted criminal, why would it be bold?' asked John.

'Wanted for what precisely?' she asked.

'Uh, he didn't actually say.'

'You didn't think to ask?'

'To be honest, after he offered so much gold, I sort of forgot to,' said John.

Bang. The side of his face hit the ground, with a little more force this time.

'Maybe you'd like to tell me?' John asked. He hoped she stopped ramming his head into the ground soon, it was really painful.

'Now you're just being stupid,' she said as she mashed the side of his face into the dirt again.

A third voice interjected, 'If you'd stop trying to scramble what little brains my compatriot has, that would be grand.'

John peered up and saw Bienia pointing her sword at the back of the woman's head.

'Gods, am I pleased to see you,' he said.

'Let him go. Don't get up.' Bienia's voice was full of the steel of command.

John felt the vice-like grip release and quickly scrambled to his feet, swaying a bit when he got there. He winced, putting his hand to the side of his face, bringing it away covered in a mixture of blood and dirt.

'It appears you have me at a disadvantage,' said the woman, maintaining a cool demeanour despite having a sword in her face.

'Yes, we do. Which of these names do we call you?' asked Bienia, showing her the list of pseudonyms.

'Forget those names, sadistic bitch is what I call her,' muttered John.

The blonde woman glanced at the list and asked 'What does it matter if you're just going to take me back to Lucien so he can kill me?'

'Kill you? Who said anything about killing you?' asked John.

'That's what he's been trying to do for the past week.'

'Well, we aren't going to kill you' – Bienia scanned the list of names, picking one at random – 'Julienne.'

'It's as good a name as any,' said Julienne.

'Isn't that something to do with slicing vegetables?' asked John.

'Be grateful I didn't slice you,' Julienne retorted.

'Did she just call me a vegetable?' asked John, sounding offended.

'She did,' said Bienia. She returned to her line of questioning. 'So, if you haven't committed a crime, why does the captain of the watch want you killed?'

'Wait a minute,' said John. 'How long were you listening?'

'Umm, long enough,' said Bienia, sounding a bit guilty.

'You just watched me get my head beaten in?' asked John, his voice rising.

'I thought you had it all under control, you know, had some sort of plan,' Bienia suggested.

'Under control? I was getting my face messed up by that sadistic bitch.' He was trying to get his alternative name for Julienne to stick.

'Hey! I'm still here you know,' said Julienne.

They both turned back to face her.

Julienne said 'I should've run for it just then, shouldn't I?'

'Probably. Back to my question. Why does the captain of the watch want you killed?' Bienia tried waving her sword around a bit in the hope of getting an answer this time.

'Because he is a lying, traitorous weasel of a man, who knows I'm on to him.'

'What do you mean, on to him?' asked John.

'Before I answer that, can I ask you two a question?'

'Ask, don't expect an answer,' said Bienia.

'What do you know of the Northern Alliance for Freedom?'

'Never heard of them. Freedom to do what exactly?' said Bienia.

'Wait, I've heard of them,' said John. 'Aren't they the gang that have been attacking tax collectors?'

'A bit more than a gang,' said Julienne. 'Their aim is independence for the north, and they don't care how they achieve it.'

John rolled his eyes. 'Politics. Never seen the point. All that effort just to install a different set of power hungry bastards at the top.'

'Quite,' Julienne said. She paused momentarily as if in thought and then obviously came to a decision about the two of them. 'I am an agent of the incumbent power hungry bastards who want to stay that way. I'll let you work out the repercussions of killing me.'

'Repercussions bad for us I'm guessing,' said Bienia.

'You guessed right,' said Julienne. 'My turn to guess. I guess that you don't have any loyalty to your employer as you haven't murdered me yet. I bet the cheapskate didn't even offer you an advance.'

'You'd be right on both counts,' said John. He had an idea where this was heading.

'My offer is simple. Work for me, and by extension King Stephen.'

This offer was met with an awkward silence as the pair just looked at her.

'You will be paid one crown a week,' said Julienne.

The pair continued to just look at her.

'Payable in advance,' said Julienne.

Bienia raised an eyebrow, holding the sword steady.

Julienne let out an exasperated sigh. 'Plus reasonable expenses.'

John looked at Bienia and shrugged. Bienia gave a small nod.

'Looks like it's a deal,' said John.

'How about lowering your sword then?' suggested Julienne. 'It will be better for employer to employee relations.'

'Oh, sorry' said Bienia, lowering her weapon. 'Bienia Ironfist, my sword is yours.'

Julienne stood up and dusted herself down before producing two gold coins from somewhere about her person. Bienia disappeared her coin faster than the eye could follow.

'Sorry about your face,' said Julienne as she handed John his coin.

He pocketed the money and also decided to apologise. 'Sorry for calling you a sadistic bitch. The name's John by the way.'

'That's alright. It wasn't entirely unjustified. I did enjoy it a bit,' said Julienne with a wink.

John wasn't really sure how to take that wink. He was feeling a little confused about his feelings where Julienne was concerned.

'So, what now?' asked Bienia, breaking the slightly uncomfortable silence.

'Now, I hideout in the woods and you two,' said Julienne, stabbing a finger at them, 'go back and tell the captain that I was killed resisting arrest. Best say it was in the woods, so you don't have to produce a body.'

'What proof can we take him?' asked John. 'Not a body part I assume.'

'Give him this,' Julienne removed a silver ring from one of the fingers of her right hand and passed it to him. It was an intricate design, a dragon looping around the finger with a small ruby inset as its eye. 'He'll recognise it. Put some of your blood on it.' She gestured at his bleeding cheek. 'That looks nasty, you might want to get it looked at,' she said helpfully.

John's hand reflexively went to his face. Yes, it was painful and still bleeding.

'I'll meet you out by the first waymarker on the road west at dusk. Make sure you aren't followed.' After giving these instructions, she turned and hurried down the street, disappearing from sight around the next corner.

John watched her go, a strange expression on his face. Bienia looked at him quizzically and shrugged her shoulders. 'Come on then, let's find a doctor.'

CHAPTER 4

John was sitting on an old wooden chair. A gaunt man in his mid-thirties, his long, lank brown hair tied back in a ponytail, was bent over him putting the finishing touches to the stitches in John's cheek. Holding his head in a fixed position, John's eyes roamed over shelves crammed full of jars of herbs and tinctures as he steadfastly tried to ignore the painful tugging of the doctor's needlework.

'What line of work are you in that gets your face messed up like this?' the doctor inquired.

'No, don't try and talk,' he admonished as John attempted to answer. A few moments later, he wiped his hands down his blood stained apron. 'All done.'

'Thanks,' said John. This will probably leave a scar he thought. Hopefully the ruggedly handsome kind, not the hideously disfigured kind. 'I'm a bounty hunter,' he added, belatedly answering the doctor's question.

'Hmph, well I dare say I'll be seeing you again. Now, can I interest you in some leeches?' The doctor gestured at some large glass jars on a wooden bench, their fleshy prisoners writhing about inside. 'Fresh in from the leech farms of Hopferwald, the finest modern medicine can provide.' He was continuing his sales patter, choosing to ignore John's pale, nauseous face.

'No thank you. I'll just take my chances.'

'Your choice, but medically speaking, you can't go wrong with a good honest leech,' said the doctor.

'You're right, it's most definitely my choice. Don't take this personally, but I hope I don't see you again.'

The doctor just harrumphed in reply and showed John the door.

'At least he didn't try and saw your head off,' said Bienia as they walked away from the small house in which the doctor ran his surgery. 'That seems to be the solution for everything for a military doctor. Axe wound in the leg? Saw it off! Chronic athlete's foot? Saw it off!'

'This modern doctoring isn't that much fun either,' said John. 'Everything is solved with a leech. Cut on your hand? Stick a leech on it! Chronic piles? Well, let's not dwell on that.'

Biena laughed loudly. 'Poor bastard leeches.' She shook her head, grinning.

'Right then. I'll be going to see Captain Marrian. I don't think he needs to know about you for the moment,' said John.

Bienia theatrically sighed, smiled and said, 'I'll be off to the pub. Enjoy your chat with the watch.'

John found the captain in his office at the watch house. Striding past the watchman, who was still sitting at his desk, he knocked twice on the captain's door and opened it without waiting for an invitation.

'Cotterill. I do hope your return means you have her in custody.'

'Not quite. She led us a merry chase into the woods.'

'She got away?'

'No. When we finally caught up with her, she resisted arrest and ended up dead.'

Marrian's eyes narrowed. 'What proof do you have?'

John dropped the silver dragon ring on the desk. He had smeared some of his blood on it as Julienne had suggested. Marrian's eyes followed the ring as it spun to a stop, a look of recognition on his face.

'It seems you are as good as you say,' said Marrian. He briefly hesitated before pulling a leather pouch from a drawer. 'As promised, six gold crowns.' He counted out the coins onto the desk.

John quickly swept up the coins and put them in a pocket.

Marrian looked at the stitches in John's cheek. 'Looks like she put up a struggle. I do hope there were no witnesses.'

'Don't worry, no-one saw the fight,' said John truthfully. 'Now if you don't mind I have gold to spend.'

He turned to leave but paused as Marrian said, 'I would appreciate it if you didn't leave town, I may have more work for you.'

'As you wish,' acquiesced John with a small nod, before hurrying out, relieved that he seemed to have pulled off the deception.

'All things considered, it's been a successful day,' said Bienia.

Bienia and John were sitting at their now usual table in

the Contented Pig Inn. It was quiet, being the middle of the afternoon. The field labourers were still out labouring and were yet to come in for their after work pint of ale.

'It's not over yet, we still need to go meet you know who,' John reminded her.

'Do we? What if we just disappeared with the coin we have?'

'Not a good idea. Captain Marrian specifically asked me not to leave town. He may suspect we didn't actually kill her. Leaving so soon would only confirm any suspicion he has.'

'True, though he only asked you to stay in town,' said Bienia. 'He doesn't even know about me.'

'Classy. You're also forgetting you know who. If she is who she says she is, and I'm inclined to believe her, then leaving Stonebridge won't help,' said John.

'True enough. I wasn't really considering leaving you in the cack you know.'

John started a smile which turned into a wince as it pulled on his stitches.

'One more for the road?' he suggested, wanting something to dull the pain.

'Of course,' said Bienia.

They ended up having two for the road before leaving. The sun was dipping towards the horizon as the pair hurried out of town along West Street.

'One of these days, I'll buy myself a horse,' said John.

'You wouldn't get me on one of those beasts. Unsafe, that's what it is.'

'Come on, let's pick up the pace. I don't want to be late.'

'Easy for you to say you long legged freak, I'm going as fast as I can.'

Bienia was almost breaking into a run beside John's long stride, her armour clanking as she moved.

'Do you ever take that armour off?' asked John.

'That's a bit forward Johnny boy,' Bienia teased, slightly breathlessly, half jogging beside him.

'I didn't mean it like that!'

Bienia laughed at his discomfort. 'I know that you daft bugger, and in answer to your question, yes. For sleeping, washing and, umm, pleasure. Not necessarily in that order.'

'Wish I'd never asked,' said John, his face reddening slightly.

They travelled the rest of the way to the marker in silence, the exertion of the pace John was setting robbing them of spare breath to speak.

After fifteen minutes it came into view, a small squat stone by the side of the road. The word Stonebridge was engraved above an arrow pointing back eastward along with the number two. The opposite arrow showed that Port Denly was thirty miles to the west, at least a full day's travel away. Looking to the west, they saw the sun disappearing behind the line of trees and the road onwards to Port Denly plunging into the darkening wood.

'Made it in time then,' said Bienia in between pulling down lungfuls of air.

'Yup,' said John tersely, his hands on his knees as he also recovered his breath.

'Pssst,' a voice came from a nearby copse of trees.

'Don't look now,' said Bienia, 'but that tree just said "Pssst".'

John turned to look.

She threw her hands in the air. 'Of course, don't listen to me. Go ahead and gawp.'

Looking closer at the trees revealed Julienne peering around a tree trunk. 'Will you two stop the comedy double act and get over here,' she said in an urgent whisper.

They hurried over as instructed. Julienne was still dressed in her black outfit, but it seemed to have picked up a distracting tear in the fabric that ran down her left hip.

'Up here,' Julienne told John. He raised his eyes from his inspection of the damage to her clothing and met her gaze. Feeling a little embarrassed he blurted out, 'Reporting as requested.'

'Did Lucien believe you?'

'He didn't seem to doubt it. The ring seemed to convince him. Oh, and this.' He touched his stitches.

'Good. Now we can proceed with the next part of the plan.'

'Plan? There's a plan?' Bienia piped up. 'Why wasn't I informed?'

Julienne ignored the interruption. 'This is a dwarven map,' she said as she produced a rolled up piece of paper from a pouch and passed it to John. 'It shows the location of a dwarven outpost on the southern border of the Hammerfist Clan lands. This outpost is the location that Derek Panely, a NAFF agent, is currently visiting.'

Bienia chuckled. 'Northern Alliance for Freedom. They didn't really think that name through.'

'All very interesting, but what does that have to do with us?' asked John.

'She wants us to go there and find out what's going on,' said Bienia.

'That's right,' said Julienne. 'You two are well placed for this task, mainly because Bienia here is the right race.'

'Sounds a bit dangerous,' said John.

'Hazard pay will apply. Just don't let him know you are on to him. I'll be watching for your return. Now get your arses back to town, you can leave tomorrow.'

CHAPTER 5

The next day found them walking again. They had passed through the farmland surrounding Stonebridge and were now walking along a narrow path that slowly climbed its way towards the fells.

'Didn't think I'd be on my way back to Hornbur quite this soon,' said Bienia.

'I've been meaning to ask you. Any dangers on the way to this outpost?'

'Apparently, there are trolls living up in the fells, but I didn't see any on the way through last time,' said Bienia, not at all reassuringly.

John looked about nervously. 'Trolls?'

'Don't worry. If there are any about, they'll know better than to mess with a dwarven shieldmaiden.'

They walked on in silence for a few more minutes before Bienia said, 'We'll get to a good campsite up ahead soon. Nice flat bit of ground and a cooking pit. If we're lucky, there'll be some wood left in the firewood shelter.'

They were lucky and soon had a fire burning in the pit. It was a couple of feet across with rocks placed all around the lip.

Bienia had quickly erected her tent and was sitting under the eaves eating a spiced sausage. She had removed her armour, giving the lie to her earlier answer about when she took it off.

John was lying on his bedroll, looking at the stars slowly disappearing behind dark, gathering clouds.

'Looks like it might rain. I don't suppose you have any spare space in that tent?' he asked hopefully.

'I still can't believe you don't have one,' said Bienia.

'Never got round to replacing it. I've always had an inn or a barn to sleep in,' said John.

'Sure, there's room for two in here. Tent rules apply. No snoring, no farting, no trying to play nug-a-nug.'

He laughed. 'I think I can manage the first two, but I'm not sure what playing nug-a-nug is.'

Bienia made a circle with her thumb and forefinger and made a lewd gesture with a finger from the other hand.

John blushed. 'I can manage that rule too.'

'Come on in then.' She moved to one side allowing him in the tent.

He got comfortable and heard Bienia crawl inside, settle down next to him and then break one of her tent rules. 'Sorry, that was the sausage.'

'Good night Bienia,' he said, trying not to gag on the unpleasant, slightly spicy, pungent smell that was now filling the tent.

'Good night Johnny boy.'

The following day started well enough. The cloud laden sky did not deliver its promised cargo of rain until late in the afternoon. At which point the day suddenly deteriorated as it came down all at once, a great deluge accompanied by a strong wind driving the cold rain into their faces.

'This is no good, we need to find some shelter!' John shouted over the wind.

'Agreed,' yelled Bienia. 'We should head over there.' She pointed to the base of a rocky crag to the right. 'Might be a cave.'

Heads bowed against the driving rain, they made their way to the rocks.

'There!' Bienia shouted, pointing again. This time at a dark and foreboding cave entrance.

John suppressed his initial trepidation at entering unknown dark holes and hurried inside. Bienia watched as he dumped his pack on the floor and pulled out his lantern and tinderbox.

It took a few attempts before the sparks lit the lantern. He stood, holding it up, throwing jagged jumping shadows which looked like crazed demons leaping from wall to ceiling and back again around the cave's interior.

Bienia looked around, a half smile on her lips, 'Well done. You've turned it from dark and slightly scary, to partially lit and terrifying.'

John laughed nervously and put the lantern on a convenient flat piece of rock.

They both shed their rain cloaks, laying them out optimistically on some rocks to dry.

'We should check how far back this goes,' said Bienia.

'Is that necessary? Can't we rest up and have some food instead?'

'Have you checked to see what this area is called on the map?'

John found the map and unrolled it, peering at it in the

lamplight. 'All of the place names are written in dwarven runes. I've no idea what they say.'

Bienia leant over his shoulder, pointing a finger at a set of angular runes next to the area on the map they were in. 'That roughly translates as "Troll fells". Now forgive me for being a bit paranoid, but I would quite like to check to see how deep this cave is.'

'Right. We'd best check the cave then.'

'You stay here and keep an eye on our bags and the entrance, I'll see how far this thing goes back,' said Bienia.

John threw a mock salute. 'Yes ma'am.'

Bienia retrieved her lantern from her pack and lit it, before picking her way carefully through the rocks, heading deeper into the cave.

As he sat at the entrance, watching the rain hammering down outside, John started to daydream about returning to Stonebridge a conquering hero. Julienne is so grateful she agrees to an intimate supper. The evening passes in delightful conversation – she laughs at all his jokes and listens in awe to his tales of bravery. Then they sit outside, looking at the stars. His arm around her, they move closer...

Suddenly his pleasant imaginings were interrupted as something clattered noisily off the cave wall and landed on the floor a few feet away. It was Bienia's lantern, now extinguished.

'To arms!' Bienia shouted as she pulled him to his feet. She then grabbed her shield before spinning around to face back, into the cave.

He turned, drew his sword, and was confronted with a hideous sight.

Bipedal, the creature stood fully eight feet tall, stooping

inside the cavern. Two black glistening orbs peered out from under long ratty hair that hung from a misshapen, lumpy head. Its bandy legs were covered in shaggy black fur, its chest and arms grey-skinned and bare. Looking at its hands, John saw razor sharp talons at the tips of each of its three fingers. It halted just out of sword reach and let out a bellowing roar. The creature's breath stank of rotten meat and its mouth was full of jagged cruel teeth.

'I'm guessing that's a troll.' John nodded towards the creature, keeping his eyes on it

'I really don't know how you do it,' said Bienia, holding her shield forward and sword up, ready to strike.

The troll did not seem eager to come much closer to the two drawn swords choosing to send another foul smelling roar their way instead.

'Well, I'm not standing like this all day,' said John. 'Attack on the count of three?'

Bienia nodded and counted off the numbers – 'One, two, three!'

On three they both lunged forward bringing their swords to bear on the awful creature.

The troll lashed out at Bienia as they attacked, its talons being caught skilfully on her shield. The force of the blow knocked her back making her trip over a rock and fall to the floor with a clatter of armour and a loud curse.

John slashed his sword down on its left arm leaving a gash that slowly pumped out thick black blood.

The creature roared in pain and stepped back, clutching at its injured arm. Bienia scrambled back to her feet, and they both watched in horror as the wound John inflicted started to close. The black blood stopped flowing as the gash disappeared and the creature surged forward again.

'Fire,' said Bienia urgently. 'We need fire.'

'You hold it off, I'll get some oil.'

'Right, hold it off he says,' Bienia muttered as she lifted her shield and moved in front of John, protecting him while he rifled through his pack.

Two more blows rained down on Bienia, the impacts absorbed by her shield held above her head.

'Got it,' said John, pulling a stoppered clay bottle from his pack.

Bienia's laboured reply was punctuated by the sounds of combat. 'Don't just stand there' – a thump echoed around the cave as a taloned hand hit her shield – 'do something!' There was a clatter as her sword deflected a razor sharp talon.

John threw the bottle at the roof of the cave above the troll. It shattered with a loud crack, and the troll was doused in lamp oil.

It let up the assault on the beleaguered shieldmaiden for a moment as the liquid stung its eyes. The respite gave Bienia enough time to grab the lit lantern from the rock shelf and hurl it directly at the beast. The lamp oil caught fire, engulfing the creature in flame. It screamed and howled in agony and started lumbering for the cavern entrance and the rain storm.

'Don't let it get out,' shouted John.

'Quick! Get behind me and push.' Biena had positioned herself in the troll's path and slammed her shield into its burning body, trying to force it back.

She was slowly being pushed back until John threw his weight behind her, and together they shoved the monster, sending it toppling onto its back where it writhed in agony.

Not wanting to leave anything to chance the two of

them fell upon it with their swords, hacking and slicing until it stopped moving and the floor was slick with its thick black blood.

'That's made a bit of a mess,' said John.

'Pongs a bit too,' said Bienia.

'Want to go find another cave?'

'Yes, but first we need to take something.'

'Take something?'

'An ear, the left to be precise,' said Bienia while sawing at the creature's ear with her boot knife.

'Isn't that a bit macabre, collecting ears?'

'It's given me an idea for a cover story at the outpost,' said Bienia. 'We're troll hunters, come to collect the trollgilt for our kill.'

'Come again?' said John, not quite following.

'Trollgilt, it's like one of your bounties, but for the left ear of trolls. My people really dislike trolls.'

After Bienia had completed her amateur ear butchery, they gathered their belongings and braved the rain to look for some shelter. They soon found a cave fifty yards or so along the base of the crag which was, to their relief, devoid of horrible beasts.

CHAPTER 6

The rain stopped just before sunrise, and the day dawned bright and crisp. According to their map, the outpost was about a day's travel away, and they resolved to reach it before nightfall. They made good time along the track, and as dusk approached the outpost came into view. It consisted of a number of wooden buildings surrounded by a sturdy looking stone wall. They could make out figures patrolling the battlements. A large wooden gate was currently open, and they hurried down the track towards it before it was closed for the night. As they got closer, a dwarven warrior stepped out to greet them. He was dressed in a chain mail hauberk and carried a huge axe over his shoulder.

'Keep quiet and follow my lead,' Bienia whispered to John. He nodded in reply.

'Halt,' the dwarf ordered. 'State your names and business.'

'Bienia Ironfist and John. We are troll hunters, and have come to collect trollgilt.' Bienia held up the severed ear as proof of her claim.

The dwarf clearly recognised her. 'Well met Bienia, a

change of career is it? You keep unusual company.' He gestured at John. 'That does not look like a troll slayer to me.'

'He may not look like much, but he has a surprisingly good sword arm.'

John looked a bit put out as the dwarf chuckled. 'Welcome back to Hornbur. You'll have to wait to collect your trollgilt. The Reckoner is busy with the Commander and another one of these tall folk.'

John and Biena exchanged a glance at this. This 'other tall folk' must be Derek Panely, meeting with the commander no less.

'Thank you, Gunter. We'll head to the ale hall for a few beers then,' said Bienia.

Gunter nodded them through the gate. They walked inside and started to head towards a large structure in the middle of the compound. To their left, John saw what looked like some enormous iron tubes mounted on wooden carts. He stopped and looked at them curiously.

'What are they?' he asked.

'Cannon,' said Bienia, sounding a little surprised.

'Cannon?'

'Siege weapons. They're used to break down gates and walls. Not sure why they've got some in Hornbur, they weren't here last week.'

'Like a battering ram?'

Bienia chuckled and said, 'No, they shoot iron balls at the enemy.' She pointed at a pyramid of iron balls stacked nearby.

'Not really following,' said John.

'Just pray you aren't near one when they're fired, your ears will be ringing for days.'

'I'll bear that in mind. Come on, let's get inside,' said John.

The hall contained several long and, to John's eyes, low tables. Some dwarves were at the tables, sitting on benches and stools, talking loudly and drinking dwarvish beer from pewter tankards. To one side, a particularly rotund dwarf served the beer from a large keg that sat raised up on wooden blocks. Smoke from an open fire and tobacco pipes filled the upper part of the hall. Against the far wall were some cots provided for any travellers staying the night to sleep on.

'When in Hornbur,' said Bienia with a grin.

'Fine, but only a couple,' said John. 'Remember why we're here.'

They approached the dwarf by the keg. His cheery eyes and rosy cheeks suggested he had been conducting some extensive quality testing of his product.

'Bienia! Back so soon?' He was already pouring a beer for her.

'Tharbor, good to see you, you old sot.' Bienia took the proffered tankard and giving him a handful of coins in exchange. 'One for the lanky fellow as well.'

Tharbor nodded and poured another measure for John; the beer sloshed over the rim as he handed it to him.

'Thanks. You two know each other then?' asked John.

Tharbor nodded enthusiastically. 'This lass drank many doughty dwarves under the table and won a few wagers on her last visit here.' Tharbor stroked his beard. 'Which was only a few days ago. What happened? No-one hiring soldiers?'

Bienia was taking a long swig of her beer as he asked

this and held a forefinger up as she continued to drain the tankard dry. She passed it back for a refill as she answered, 'I decided troll slaying is where it's at. Hired the boy here to help out.' She jerked a thumb in John's direction.

Some of John's beer seemed to go down the wrong way as she made this assertion.

'Can't handle his ale though,' Bienia remarked as he was coughing and spluttering.

She looked around the ale hall as if trying to spot someone. 'None of the lads from last time are here?' she asked, taking the cup passed to her by Tharbor.

'No, they've been relieved. These soldiers are fresh from the fortress at Karrick,' he paused before continuing in a thoughtful tone, 'thinking of some sort of contest?' Tharbor's eyes gleamed mischievously.

'It'd be rude not to.'

'Right, I'll get the giant drinking horns,' said Tharbor eagerly. 'I think I may have a little wager on the outcome.'

John pulled Bienia to one side as Tharbor went off in search of his epic drinking equipment.

'Remember why we're here,' he whispered.

'I remember. I'm going to create a distraction so you can slip out to find Derek. Look in the big grand looking building near the north wall, that's where the commander conducts business,' said Bienia.

She shoved the troll ear into his hands, 'take this, in case you're stopped.'

'Thanks for consulting me on the plan,' said John.

'Think nothing of it,' said Bienia.

'It would've been nice to talk it over before we're in the sodding middle of it.'

'Can I pretend there was no time?'

Further discussion on the merits of holding a forward planning session was curtailed as Tharbor returned carrying a pair of large drinking horns that looked like they may have come from a woolly mammoth. He banged an empty cup against the side of the keg.

'May I have your attention please!' he yelled.

The other dwarves in the ale hall stopped their conversations and turned to see what the fuss was about. Their eyes lit up as they caught sight of the massive drinking horns.

'It's contest time!' Tharbor exclaimed as he started filling the horns.

Bienia had climbed up onto a nearby table. 'Who will challenge me? I have a gold coin,' she held a gold crown between finger and thumb, 'which says I can drain this horn faster than any dwarf here.'

The assembled dwarves erupted in a hubbub of conversation, then one of them stepped forward. He was dressed in a grubby grey tunic and had a beard that was plaited into two spikes with bone beads on the end. 'I'll take your money,' he said, rolling his sleeves up.

Bienia smiled broadly and jumped down from the table, her armour clanking as she landed.

Tharbor handed each of them a drinking horn and then counted down: 'Three, two, one, drink!'

All eyes were on the beer guzzling pair as John quietly slipped outside.

It was dark outside the ale hall, the only light provided by the moon and a few torches mounted on posts hammered into the ground. The gate was now closed for the night and the only movement to be seen was that of the sentries pacing the walls.

John walked around the hall and towards the north of the compound. Near the north wall, as Bienia had said, there was a two storey building with a large double door. There were numerous windows spaced around the structure, their wooden shutters closed. Light was bleeding out from a set of shutters on the ground floor. John figured this was where the meeting was taking place and moved close enough to hear voices within.

'We are agreed then,' said a deep male voice. Listening to the accent, John deduced that it was a dwarven voice, probably the commander.

'Agreed, further payment will be made when you deliver the final shipment,' said a second male voice. This time, the words were spoken in the distinctive tones of someone born and bred in the north of Asterland.

'I'm surprised you haven't used what we sent you already,' said the dwarf.

'We will be using it all at once to increase the element of surprise and' – there was an ominous chuckle – 'for a bigger effect.'

'All of it? That's going to be a big effect alright. We'll be able to see it from Hornbur.'

'We do intend to make an impression.'

'Well, I dare say you will. Good luck Mister Panely.'

'Thank you, commander. We will be in touch with you after the deed is done.'

John heard footsteps and an internal door open. The light was extinguished, and the door slammed shut. Having heard all he usefully could, John decided to go back to the ale hall so he could discuss their next move with Bienia. As he was rounding the corner of the building, he heard the front door open and quickly flattened himself against the wall. Peering carefully around the corner he saw a clean-shaven man of average height and build, his long, dark hair tied back. The man closed the door and walked towards the ale hall. He was dressed in good quality clothes, was carrying a backpack and wore a sword at his waist. That must be Panely, thought John. He watched the man walk out of sight before he left his hiding place and followed Panely to the ale hall

John re-entered the ale hall to find Bienia just finishing up another drinking contest. This time it was versus a fat dwarf with a huge blonde beard. The other dwarves were banging their cups on the table in a steady rhythm. Bienia beat the challenger with a full second to spare, holding the horn upside down over her head to prove it was empty. The audience erupted in a cheer as the loser grudgingly handed over a gold coin while putting up with the teasing of his comrades. Bienia pocketed the coin, bowed dramatically, and came over to talk to John.

'Well, I just made a few gold and drank plenty of good beer. How did you do?'

He glanced around to make sure no-one was listening.

'I overheard a conversation between the commander and our friend over there.' He subtly indicated Panely, who was sitting alone at the far end of one of the tables.

'And?'

John repeated what he had heard and then said, 'I'm thinking we need to find out what this shipment is.'

Bienia had started to look uncomfortable while John was talking and by the time he had finished, she was shuffling from one foot to the other.

'Let's talk about this in a minute, I just, er, need to go do something outside,' she said and hurried out of the ale hall. John waited impatiently until she returned a few minutes later with a satisfied look on her face.

'Better?' asked John.

'Much. I was thinking, we can follow Panely when he leaves the outpost and beat whatever he knows out of him.'

'No good. We're supposed to be doing this on the quiet remember. He mustn't suspect.'

'That leaves finding out from the commander,' said Bienia.

'Do you think he'll tell us?'

'Perhaps. I can only ashk.' Bienia was starting to slur her words.

'Can you ask him in a roundabout way? We need to be subtle.'

'You worry too much.' She paused as a hiccup escaped. 'Ish fine.'

John noticed that Bienia's eyes had taken on a glassy sheen, and she was sweating a little more than usual.

'Exactly how many contests did you win?' he asked.

'Four, or washit five?' Bienia weaved unsteadily from side to side.

'Gods, I was only gone ten minutes.'

Bienia giggled like a little school-dwarf. 'Hash I been a naughty shieldmaiden?' she said, hiccuping again to punctuate her question. She lurched, lost her balance, and fell against John.

'Easy, I got you,' John said. 'Let's get you to bed.'

'Ish thash an offer?' she slurred, giving John's posterior an experimental squeeze. 'Mushcular.'

45

John let out an involuntary yelp. 'Hey! Cut that out.'

He manoeuvred her to the visitor cots, the trip punctuated by inebriated ramblings on the nature of true friendship. He picked one out and unceremoniously dumped her. She collapsed onto the cot heavily, and almost immediately started snoring loudly.

'I think tonight you can sleep with your armour on,' John told the now comatose dwarf.

The following morning Bienia woke to the smell of cooking sausages. She carefully opened an eye to see several sausages sizzling on a grill over the fire. Tharbor was next to them wearing a stained apron, occasionally turning one. John was sitting on a bench, eating. He saw her eye open and smiled at her. 'Morning! Breakfast?' he asked.

Bienia hauled herself to a sitting position and looked about for her clothes and armour. She realised she was still wearing them and stood up. 'Some food might settle my stomach,' she said in a low voice.

Tharbor deftly lifted a sausage from the grill by piercing it on the end of a fork and slapped it on a pewter plate which he then passed to Bienia. 'One of my speciality sausages, guaranteed to cure what ails you.'

'Panely left first thing,' John told her after she joined him on the bench. 'He was headed back to Asterland. I tried talking to him to see if he'd let anything slip, but he wasn't very talkative.'

Bienia grunted as she chewed and swallowed a bit of sausage. 'He was unlikely to just say what he was up to.'

'On the bright side, he didn't seem to doubt my troll hunter story, especially when I showed him the ear.'

'We'll see the Reckoner and cash it in after I've finished eating,' said Bienia.

'Then we can see if the commander is more forthcoming about the reason for Panely's visit,' said John, finishing outlining the morning's plan of action.

After breakfast, they went to visit the Reckoner in the two storey building John had been eavesdropping at the previous night. They were shown into his counting room. It was a grand room, its walls decorated with shields bearing the crossed hammers of the Hammerfist Clan and the mounted head of a grizzly bear. On the large table in the centre of the room were a scattering of documents and a few stacks of different coin denominations. The Reckoner himself was an older dwarf with a luxuriant grey beard. He was fussing with some of the pieces of paper when they entered.

'Well met. We're here for trollgilt,' said Bienia, holding up the ear.

'Yes, yes. Is it just the one?' The Reckoner walked over and peered at the ear.

'Only one, that's right,' said Bienia. As this exchange was taking place, John happened to glance at a piece of paper on the table and was surprised to see Derek Panely's name on it. He quickly checked to see if the Reckoner was looking before he grabbed it, hurriedly hiding it by cramming it down his trousers.

The Reckoner took a few moments to satisfy himself that this was indeed a troll's left ear before he said, 'Very well, the payment is three gold coins per left ear.'

The pair thanked him and left after collecting their payment.

'Now for the commander,' said Bienia.

'That may not be necessary,' said John.

Bienia frowned and opened her mouth to say something.

'I'll tell you more when we have some privacy,' said John, pre-empting her question.

Once outside John led Bienia to a secluded corner of the compound, away from prying eyes. He stuck his hand down his trousers to retrieve the paper.

'What? No, no, I'm not—' said Bienia.

John pulled the paper out from its hiding place.

'Thank the Gods,' Bienia said, looking relieved.

John flattened out the paper, and they both looked at it in more detail. It appeared to be a purchase order for a rather large supply of dwarvish blasting powder.

Bienia let out a low whistle. 'That's a lot of powder. Expensive.'

'This is what we came for,' said John. 'We need to leave and get back to Julienne.'

Bienia nodded agreement, and they hurried back to the ale hall. Once there, they quickly gathered their belongings. Tharbor was still standing next to the fire, grilling his sausages and noticed their preparations. 'Leaving so soon?'

'We got our trollgilt, time to go earn some more. Those trolls won't slay themselves,' said Bienia.

'True enough. Well, I'll look forward to your return,' said Tharbor, then he turned to John. 'You're not all that bad for a man John, good hunting.'

'Thanks, Tharbor, be seeing you,' said John.

Bienia clasped Tharbor's forearm. 'Until the next time.'

With their farewells complete, the pair walked out of the ale hall. Gunter was leaning on his axe as he watched them approach. He simply nodded at them as they passed through the gate and took the track south, heading back through the Troll Fells and towards Asterland's northern border.

CHAPTER 7

The journey south was uneventful. There were no torrential rain storms; the weather stayed boringly calm. There were no troll attacks; they stayed out of dark caves. John realised he forgot to buy a tent at the dwarven outpost; Bienia let him share hers.

They approached Stonebridge as the sun was setting, lighting the patchy clouds with a vivid red.

'I wonder if the captain noticed I was gone,' said John.

'We'll find out soon enough,' said Bienia.

They walked directly to the Contented Pig and arranged rooms for the night before settling at what had become their usual table.

'What now?' asked Bienia.

'Not sure. Julienne said she'd watch for our return. I assume she'll contact us.'

'We should have a couple of beers while we wait.'

'It would be rude not to,' said John.

After several polite pints, they said their good nights and retired to their rooms.

John entered his room and closed the door. As he looked around the room, he was alarmed to see a dark figure step from the shadowy corner of the room. John tensed, his hand instinctively going to his sword, but then relaxed when he recognised the shapely form of Julienne. He noticed the distracting tear in her clothing had been repaired.

'Up here,' Julienne told him.

John looked back up at her face and blushed, hoping the gloom covered his embarrassment.

'You're back,' she said, stating the obvious. 'What do you have to report?'

John pulled the purloined purchase order from a pocket. 'This. We don't know what they're planning, but it's going to be explosive.'

Julienne took the proffered document. 'I can't read in the dark. A little light?'

'Right.' John pulled out his flint and steel and lit the candle on the bedside table.

Julienne sat on the bed and read the purchase order by the flickering candle light. She frowned. 'This isn't good. Did you see the date on this? Four weeks ago. Whatever plan they've put in motion is well underway.'

'I didn't manage to get anything out of Panely when I talked to him.'

'You talked to Panely?' she said sharply.

'Uh, yes. Told him I was a troll hunter, asked him a few vague questions.'

'That wasn't very smart.'

'He wasn't suspicious, he believed my troll hunter story.'

'You don't think he is going to find it strange when this troll hunter shows up in Stonebridge? Almost as if he is being followed?' Julienne asked.

'I didn't think about that,' John admitted.

Julienne sat, thinking for a moment and came to a decision. 'We're leaving tonight. My sources have reported that something is being planned in Port Denly. I'd leave you here, but we can't risk Panely seeing you.'

'Sorry,' said John.

'Let's go.' Julienne pushed past him on her way to the door. 'Which room is the dwarf in?'

Five minutes later, they were jogging down the streets of Stonebridge on their way to West Street and the road to Port Denly. The town was quiet; the moonlit streets were empty of people at this time of night. Bienia was lagging behind, muttering something about long legged freaks when John and Julienne rounded the corner onto West Street and almost walked into two watchmen. Everyone looked at each other for a few seconds. John recognised Captain Marrian. He also saw recognition on Marrian's face.

'Hello, Lucien,' said Julienne, politely greeting Marrian using his first name. John noticed that her hand was resting on the hilt of her sword. The two watchmen tensed, moving their hands to their weapons.

'I didn't expect to see you again Cassandra,' said Marrian.

John was momentarily puzzled before he realised Cassandra must be one of Julienne's pseudonyms.

'Oh? You know I love to turn up when you least expect it,' said Julienne. Her hand didn't move from her sword.

'This is particularly unexpected.' Marrian glared at John. 'Looks like I made a bad choice with the hired help.'

'You've always been particularly incompetent. How

long did you trust me for? Was it one year or two? I forget.'

Marrian's face darkened, and he drew his sword with a low steel hiss. 'Looks like I get to kill you after all, along with this traitorous dog.'

Bienia heard the sounds of weapons being drawn from around the corner and stopped for a moment to ready her sword and shield. She had not been spotted yet and intended to make the most of the element of surprise.

'Come on Lucien, try me,' taunted Julienne. She had adopted a fighting stance, sword in her right hand and a dagger in her left.

Marrian growled in fury, raised his sword and slashed viciously down at Julienne. She parried expertly with the dagger and lunged forward with her sword. The lunge was into space as Marrian twisted out of the way, moving back to a guard position. Meanwhile, John was clashing swords with the second watchman, each probing for a gap in the other's defences.

Bienia watched from around the corner, taking in the scene of concentrated combat. She held back, waiting for an opportunity to strike. It soon came when Marrian turned his back on her hiding place. Suppressing her natural desire to shout a battle cry, Bienia silently moved forward and chopped her sword into Marrian's neck. Blood fountained out of the wound as he suddenly looked surprised, and then fell to his knees before finally collapsing face down, a crimson pool forming around his head.

Seeing his Captain lying in a pool of blood proved too much for the remaining watchman; he turned and started running down the street.

John lowered his sword, letting him go.

Julienne, however, had other ideas. She swapped her dagger into her right hand, drew back her arm and threw the blade straight into the retreating man's back. He let out a scream and fell to the cobblestones, his sword clattering loudly as it skittered across the street. Julienne quickly ran over to the prone man and retrieved her dagger from his back. She lifted the injured man's head up by his hair and drew the dagger across his throat. Julienne looked up and saw the horrified look on John's face. 'No witnesses,' she said tersely. 'Now, time to run.'

Bienia grimly nodded as she wiped her blade clean on the dead captain's tunic. John recovered his composure, and the three of them ran towards West Street leaving the two still warm corpses behind them.

They had made it past the first waymarker on the road to Port Denly before the bodies were discovered and a hue and cry started up. They could hear the distant shouts of the watch being roused to search for the killers of their captain.

'Quickly, not far to the woods,' Julienne urged them on.

They ran down the road with renewed vigour, spurred on by the sounds of the town watch bell ringing behind them and soon reached the tree line, following the dark tree-shrouded road into the wood.

They slowed to a walk and got their breath back before John said, 'We should get off this road. They'll be up here on horseback soon.'

Bienia and Julienne agreed, so they followed the next small trail that branched off the road. After following the trail for about a quarter of a mile, it opened out into a small clearing. A large pile of wood was stacked next to where they entered the clearing, and a well built wooden hut stood in the middle, illuminated by the moonlight.

'Woodcutter's hut,' said John, 'do we see if anyone is at home?'

'As we need somewhere to stay, and I'm the only one with a tent, yes,' said Bienia.

'Not room for three in the tent?' asked Julienne.

Bienia shook her head. 'Two is intimate, three would be indecent.'

'So, do we just go and knock?' asked John.

Julienne shrugged. 'Sure. I'll do the talking.'

They walked up to the hut. Julienne stepped up to the door and rapped her knuckles on it three times. They saw the shutter on the window next to the door open a crack. A nervous male voice, slightly muffled by the door, said, 'Who are you? What do you want? I warn you, I have an axe!'

'We mean you no harm. We are just three simple travellers caught out with nowhere to sleep tonight,' said Julienne, pitching her voice to be soft and soothing.

'Stonebridge isn't far, go and bother them,' responded the voice, 'I wasn't joking about the axe you know.'

'Alas, my friend is sick, and cannot travel any further tonight, can you please help us?'

'Sick? What sort of sick? Not that Wan-Feng fever is it? If it is you can just bugger off.'

'No. He has a malady of the stomach that saps his strength, it's not catching,' said Julienne. Then when that did not elicit a response, she said, 'We can pay.'

Those seemed to be the three magic words. 'Why didn't you say that in the first place?'

They heard a wooden bar being removed from the

inside of the door followed by the rattle of a key in a lock. The door opened to reveal a six-foot man who filled his simple homespun clothes with his muscular frame. He had a bald head, a big bushy beard and was holding a long woodcutter's axe in his right hand.

He introduced himself. 'My name's Colin. You are?'

'This is Freya and poor, sick Bartholomew. I'm Charlotte.'

John realised he was Bartholomew and whispered to Bienia, 'Why do I get to be the sick one?'

Bienia shrugged, stifling a laugh.

'You mentioned payment?' prompted Colin.

'Ah, yes. Julienne pulled a gold coin from somewhere. John still couldn't quite figure out where she kept them.

Colin's eyes widened at the sight of the gold, and he hurriedly moved to one side, 'Come in, come in, you are most welcome.'

They trooped through the door and into a large living area. It contained a table, chairs and an iron stove which was radiating warmth. There was a wooden door, which was slightly ajar, leading to what looked like a bedroom.

'Sorry about the unfriendly welcome,' said Colin, 'I thought you were the tax collectors. They've been bleeding us dry.'

'As you can see, not tax collectors.' Julienne gestured at Bienia and John.

Bienia nudged John and whispered, 'Aren't you supposed to be ill?'

John let out a theatrical moan, clutching his stomach.

'You sound in a bad way,' said Colin as he moved a chair out from the table for John. 'Here, sit yourself down. Are you hungry? I have some bread I can spare. Not for

Bartholomew of course, wouldn't do your stomach any good I reckon.'

John groaned again, this time in dismay at not getting anything to eat.

As the others sat down and ate the slightly stale bread, Colin continued complaining about the amount of tax he had to pay. 'It's just not right. All that money we Northerners pay, going to all those fat nobles down south. Those Northern Alliance fellows have the right of it.'

Julienne raised an eyebrow as she listened.

Colin interrupted his monologue to lean over and open the door on the stove. He peered inside, and said 'Need more wood.' He then stood up and left the hut, presumably to get some more fuel from the woodpile.

'He's a NAFF sympathiser, we should get rid of him,' said Julienne putting her piece of bread down.

'Hold on a minute, you mean kill him?' asked John.

'Yes, kill him,' said Julienne. 'No witnesses remember? He'll give us away if the watch come knocking.'

'No. I'll not be a party to cold-blooded murder,' said John.

'You don't have to, I'll do it. If that's what you're worried about,' said Julienne. She sounded genuinely puzzled about John's objection.

'That's not what I'm worried about. What I'm worried about is ending the life of a perfectly decent man, whose only crime is thinking he pays a bit too much tax. Which, incidentally, I can fully sympathise with.'

'The minute the watch turn up he'll tell them everything he knows. We have to silence him.'

'Bee, back me up,' John pleaded with Bienia.

'I'm with John on this. No killing,' said Bienia.

Julienne raised her hands and said, 'Alright. I surrender. Have it your way.'

At this point Colin re-entered the hut, effectively stopping any further discussion about his potential demise. He dumped the pile of logs he was carrying onto the floor, opened the stove door and added one to the fire.

'Nice bread,' said Bienia, breaking the awkward silence that had descended on the room.

'I bought it from Mrs Wiggins in Stonebridge. She bakes a good loaf,' said Colin.

John saved everyone from any further small talk by announcing, 'There's a couple of horsemen coming down the trail.' He had opened the window shutters a crack and had been idly looking outside.

'It's as busy as Port Denly coach house here tonight,' grumbled Colin, moving over to the window and peering out.

'Looks like the watch, what are they doing out here?' said Colin.

'They're after us for...' John paused, mind racing for something to say.

'Evading taxes,' said Bienia, finishing for him.

'Are they now?' said Colin belligerently. 'You take yourselves into the other room, I'll give them a talking to they won't forget.'

The three of them moved into the adjoining bedroom, leaving Colin getting worked up about the iniquities of taxation and the common man. Julienne gently closed the door and looked around the small room. A smile appeared on her face when she saw a window was on the opposite side of the hut from the front door.

'Right, out the window and steal their horses while

they're distracted with our militant woodcutter friend,' she said, surprising both Bienia and John with a newfound level of detail in her planning.

John gave Bienia a boost through the window and then followed her out into the moonlit night. He turned and watched appreciatively as Julienne climbed through the window backwards. Meanwhile, Bienia was looking somewhere more productive, around the corner of the hut. She saw that the watchmen's horses were tied to a tree near the edge of the clearing and relayed this information to the others.

Julienne was crouched beside the window, listening to voices from inside the hut. 'They're inside. Let's move.'

The trio quickly ran across the clearing to where two horses were tethered. Julienne quickly untied one of the horses and expertly swung herself into the saddle. John took a little more time getting himself into the saddle of the second horse. Bienia looked up at the horses dubiously. 'I'm not sure about this.'

John reached down to offer a hand up to Bienia. Despite her trepidation, Bienia grabbed John's hand and was hoisted onto the horse behind him. She wrapped her arms around his middle, clinging on with a vice-like grip as if her life depended on it.

'You don't need to hold on so hard,' gasped John, worried she might crack one of his ribs.

'Sorry,' said Bienia, relaxing her grip a little.

'Let's ride,' said Julienne, urging her stolen horse into motion.

John finally cajoled his mount into movement, following Julienne. They left the clearing at a trot accompanied by the sounds of armour clanking and a stream of colourful invectives as Bienia was jostled around on the back of the horse.

CHAPTER 8

Several hours later, having made good their escape from the watch, they crested a hill and arrived at the last waymarker, two miles from Port Denly. Julienne brought her horse to a halt and raised her arm, signalling that John should also stop. She dismounted with an easy grace and slapped the horse's hindquarters, sending it back into the woods. Bienia's attempt to dismount was not so graceful, sliding down the back of John's horse into an ungraceful heap on the floor. She picked herself up, placed her hands on the base of her spine and arched her back. Giving the horse's hindquarters a baleful glare she said, 'If I ever, ever get on one of those Gods forsaken things again, it will be too soon.'

John grinned at her obvious discomfort as he dismounted, before sending his horse on its way back into the woods.

He turned to face in the direction of Port Denly and let out a low whistle. From this vantage point, he could see the many torches and lanterns of the city splashing patches of light across the night landscape and the moonlight shimmering on the dark waters of the Western Ocean. A formidable stone wall completely encircled the city, protecting it from would-be attackers.

'Big,' he said, somewhat superfluously.

'We'll wait until morning and enter Merchant Gate with the rest of the early arrivals,' said Julienne.

'I was hoping to get some sleep.' John rubbed his eyes and then qualified his hope, 'In a bed.'

'If we go in now while it's the middle of the night, we'll be remembered,' said Julienne, 'and worse, remembered when the Stonebridge watch reports the fugitives who killed their captain.'

'Nothing's ever bloody simple,' said John.

'Not usually, no. Come on, let's get to the gate and find somewhere to wait until dawn.'

After spending an hour walking cross country, they reached Merchant Gate on the southern side of the city. Julienne picked a small copse of trees not too far from the road and not too close to the gate in which to wait. Bienia quickly settled down, starting to softly snore moments after wedging herself between a couple of tree roots.

Julienne looked at the dwarf and smiled, shaking her head. 'Try and get some sleep, I'll keep watch.'

'I don't know how she does it either,' said John.

Julienne clapped him on the back companionably, then settled into a position on the edge of the copse where she could keep an eye on the road.

John sighed, then spent what was left of the night lying on the cold, uncomfortable ground failing to get any sleep.

In the morning the three of them saw a steady flow of people from the surrounding area entering the city via Merchant Gate. The name Merchant Gate understated things a little. It was, in fact, a large stone gatehouse with crenellated battlements and arrow slits spaced at regular intervals. With the hoods of their cloaks up and their heads down, they stepped onto the road and followed a cart laden with turnips.

Two bored looking watchmen were leaning on their spears, watching people enter, but making no move to stop or question anyone. The three of them soon passed underneath a raised portcullis and through the gatehouse itself.

Looking up, John could see several murder holes which defenders could use to pour boiling hot oil down on any attackers who made it through the first portcullis. Even though he wasn't part of an attacking army, he felt safer once they had walked out of the gatehouse, passing under the second raised portcullis.

Julienne led them purposefully through streets starting to fill with people, all going about their daily business. They soon reached an inn with a hand-painted sign of a majestic eagle, its wings extended. The words 'The Spread Eagle' had been scrawled in black paint underneath the bird.

'Finally, a bed,' John said as they entered.

The innkeeper was a large, jolly, and above all, loud man. 'Lucinda! It's good to see you again girl!' he bellowed as he caught sight of the new arrivals.

Lucinda was, of course, another of Julienne's pseudonyms.

'Leo! How could I stay away? I've been missing your delicious meat pies.' Julienne had switched from looking bone tired to a lively, cheerful demeanour without missing a beat.

'Breakfast?' asked Leo. He started to pre-emptively lay three sets of cutlery on a table.

'The works please, and three rooms.'

'Right you are. I'll ask Lily to see to your rooms, then bring you your food.'

'Thank you, Leo.' Julienne beamed a smile at him.

Once Leo had bustled off she let the energetic, cheerful façade fall away and slumped back in her chair, her exhaustion obvious.

'Right. Let's eat then get some sleep,' said Julienne. 'We'll meet back here when we've rested and discuss our next move.'

John and Bienia just nodded in response, and they all sat in a tired, stretched silence as they waited for breakfast.

Once they had eaten, Leo showed them to their rooms. They were all on the first floor and had windows facing towards the main street below.

John closed the shutters in his room, shutting out the sun and some of the noise of the street outside. He undressed and lay on the bed, the low background hubbub of the city slowly lulling him to sleep.

John was roused from his slumber by a commotion outside the inn. He sat up and held his head in his hands for a few moments, feeling the rough stitches in his cheek, before opening the shutters to see what all the shouting was about. In the street below he saw a squad of soldiers, all carrying halberds and wearing chain mail and a yellow surcoat adorned with a black rearing horse. They were clearing the road of the peasantry, shoving them aside if shouting did not work. Behind them rode a man dressed in fine riding clothes who carried a shield bearing the same symbol as the soldier's surcoats. Obviously their liege lord. Accompanying him were several others on horseback, members of his household and other hangers on John presumed. He watched the procession slowly pass by the inn before deciding it was time to get dressed and go downstairs. He had slept all morning judging from the position of the sun in the sky. It was time to find lunch.

The common room now contained other customers who were eating and drinking. A low hum of conversation filled the room. He spotted Bienia and Julienne at the same table that they had used at breakfast time. They both had a plateful of some sort of pie and potatoes covered in a thick gravy which they were eating with obvious relish. John's stomach began to rumble.

'You woke up at last,' Bienia said as he sat down next to them.

'Thanks to some nobleman barging his way through the city,' said John.

'Which nobleman?' Julienne asked, in between chewing mouthfuls of food.

'Don't know. His shield had a black horse on a yellow background.'

'Lord Rychard,' said Julienne. 'He must be here to prepare for King Stephen's visit.'

'The King is coming here?' John asked, sounding surprised.

'Yes, and I need to report what we have discovered to Lord Rychard,' Julienne said, 'and I'd better go now.'

Julienne pushed her plate towards John. 'Here finish this. You two stay put and stay out of trouble.' She stood up and brushed pie crumbs off of her tunic. 'I'm going to the keep. I'll be back in an hour.'

John watched her make her way through the inn on her way to the door. He enjoyed the easy grace of her movement as she threaded her way around the tables, although in light of her, frankly, murderous tendencies, the fact that he seemed to still be attracted to her worried him a little. With an internal sigh, he took a sip of his ale.

'Stay out of trouble, what does she mean by that?' asked Bienia as she drained her tankard of ale.

John eyed the empty tankard. 'Probably no drinking competitions.'

'Spoilsport.' She yawned and stretched, lifting her arms above her head then said, 'So this King what's his name is important is he?'

'King Stephen, he's the ruler of Asterland. All the nobles swear fealty to him, his word is absolute law.' John punctuated this summary of Asterland's feudal political system by cramming a whole potato into his mouth.

'How did he get to be king?' she asked.

There was a pause while he chewed and swallowed. 'His father, Alfred, was king, and his father before him and so on. The Gods have blessed his family, giving them divine right to rule.'

'Sounds a bit barmy to me. That's not how the dwarven High King is chosen.'

'How does it work then?' asked John.

'The clan chiefs take turns every four years. I mean yes, technically he's in charge, but in reality, he just enjoys the prestige and free beer before handing over to his successor.'

'How do they decide who goes next?' John frowned.

'They have a vote,' Bienia said. She signalled that she wanted another ale by lifting her tankard towards Leo.

'A vote?' John was shocked, almost scandalised.

Bienia nodded. 'Of course, don't you lot vote for mayors or something?'

'No, they're obviously appointed by their liege lord,' John described what he thought was a common sense arrangement.

Their discussion was interrupted by Leo refilling Bienia's tankard and depositing a second in front of John.

'You two known Lucinda long?' Leo asked.

John hesitated for a moment before he remembered this was the name Leo had called Julienne when they had arrived.

'Oh ages, we go way back,' said John, exaggerating outrageously.

'She's a good northern lass is that one. You're in town for the King's visit I suppose?' Leo gestured at the tables full of customers. 'We haven't been this busy for a long time.'

'The King's visit is good for business then?'

'About all he's good for,' said Leo. 'Not a patch on his father. Now there was a man who cared for all of the people, including us northerners.'

John mumbled his agreement before taking a gulp of ale.

'I'll leave you two alone to finish your pie. Enjoy!'

Bienia looked at John significantly as Leo left to clear empty plates and tankards from the tables. 'He's not keen on the King then.'

'I wonder who he thinks Julienne, or should I say, Lucinda is?' John absently scratched his head. 'He seemed happy enough to talk down the King once he thought we were old friends of hers.'

'We can ask her when she's back.'

After they had finished their pie and potatoes, the pair sat back in their seats and enjoyed the feeling of being full of food for a few minutes.

'What do we do until the boss gets back?' asked Bienia.

'Stay here and stay out of trouble.'

Bienia sighed. 'Right, no drinking contests.'

They sat in silence for a few seconds before she pulled a small, battered leather case from her pocket. 'So, John. Are you familiar with the game Beggar's Five?'

'No. Is it some sort of card game?' John eyed the leather case suspiciously.

'I'll teach you.' She pulled some well-used playing cards from the case and started to expertly shuffle them.

'Let me guess, it involves betting?'

'You've heard of it then?' Bienia asked innocently.

He laughed. 'Come on then. Let's see how much I can lose before Julienne gets back.'

John had found out just how much he could lose after playing for a couple of hours. There was a big pile of copper pennies and silver shillings in front of Bienia, while in front of John was a meagre stack of eleven pennies.

'Well, I don't think I'm all that good at this game,' said John.

'You've done quite well for a beginner,' said Bienia, blatantly exaggerating his skill as she scooped her winnings from the table.

John chuckled briefly and then looked serious as he asked, 'Shouldn't Julienne be back by now? She said she would be back in an hour and you've been taking my money for longer than that.'

'You're right, perhaps we should go and look for her,' said Bienia.

'She went to the keep to see Lord Rychard. We should start there.'

CHAPTER 9

'There's the keep,' said Bienia, pointing. John's eyes followed her finger and saw the imposing stone structure towering over the roofs of the buildings to the north. They walked through the afternoon crowds, trying as best they could to head for the keep. Eventually, the street they were following spilt out into a large square. In the centre of the square was a fountain, water splashing down a pair of granite dolphins. The keep was situated on the far side of the square, its gate open and guarded by four city watchmen who looked much more alert than the two they had encountered earlier that morning at Merchant Gate. They were talking to visitors before they allowed them inside the keep.

'Do we just walk in?' asked Bienia.

'I'll go, you stay here,' said John. 'There aren't many dwarves in these parts, they might ask some awkward questions.'

Bienia looked around the square. He was right, she was the only dwarf in the square, and they hadn't seen any others since arriving in the city.

'Makes sense I suppose. I'll sit here and wait.' She sat on the fountain's rim.

John put his hand on her shoulder and said, 'If I'm not back in an hour...' He stopped, unsure of what to say next.

Bienia put her hand on his. 'Good luck John. Don't be too long. Who knows what mischief I'll get up to left on my own.'

John withdrew his hand, smiled nervously and strode towards the gates, trying to look as if he was supposed to be there.

A burly watchman stepped in front of him as he approached the open gate.

'Halt, state your business,' said the watchman.

Looking past the guard, John could see a large hallway. There were many people inside bustling about. He noticed that some of them wore surcoats bearing the black horse on a yellow background of Lord Rychard.

'I'm with Lord Rychard's party, returning with a message,' he said with as much authority as he could muster.

'Very well,' said the watchman, waving him through, apparently not detecting John's brazen deception.

Relieved he hadn't been questioned further, John walked into the hallway and looked around. There were two sets of stone stairs, one to his left and one to his right. They led up to a pair of balconies which ran the length of the hallway. On the ground floor, doors were regularly spaced along each wall, and the hallway ended at a final set of heavy iron-bound wooden doors. He saw the men he had spotted earlier wearing surcoats displaying Lord Rychard's heraldic device walking up the left set of stairs, so he decided to follow them. When he reached the top, he saw they had entered another door that led off of the balcony. Standing by this door was an armed guard who was also wearing one of the distinctive yellow surcoats.

John walked up to the man and coughed, 'Excuse me, I need to see Lord Rychard.'

The guard looked him up and down. 'And you are?'

'An agent of the crown with important information for Lord Rychard.' John decided to tell the truth. After all, Julienne had been coming to report to Rychard.

'Is that so?' The man eyed John sceptically.

As John was trying to come up with something more convincing to say, he saw the guard suddenly snap to attention. Turning, he recognised Lord Rychard himself coming up the stairs accompanied by more soldiers. He was six feet tall and broad-shouldered, had a neatly trimmed beard and a full head of brown hair.

'My Lord,' said John, 'I need to speak with you on a matter of some urgency.'

Lord Rychard seemed surprised by this sudden outburst from what looked like a common soldier.

'What's that? Who is this man?' He directed this question at the guard who was still standing to attention.

'Says he's an agent of the crown my Lord.'

'Did he now? In that case, he'd better come inside and tell me what's so blasted urgent.'

'Yes my Lord,' responded the guard, stepping to one side.

Rychard barked the order, 'Follow me!' and then passed through the door without checking to see if John had obeyed.

John did obey, hurrying after the Lord as he strode through a well-appointed reception room into another room that contained a single long table and chairs. A map of Asterland and the surrounding lands was on the table, held in place by a couple of wine goblets and a silver candlestick.

John looked at the map with interest. It was embellished with pictures of cavorting sea monsters beyond the Sunset Isles in the Western Ocean; typical filler when the map maker had no knowledge of the area. In contrast, the southern border forts of Asterland were all marked and named in a neat script, from Fort Horst on the west coast all the way to Fort Pitt nestled in the foothills of the Spiky mountain range to the east.

To the south of these stalwart fortifications, the Pockveld was an empty expanse on the map, its name written in large, bold, flowing letters. No place names there; the inhabitants were nomadic and did not form permanent settlements.

Finally, his eyes were drawn to the north of the Kingdom and the familiar names Stonebridge, Port Denly and beyond them, the Troll Fells and the Silver Hills, home of the dwarven clans.

Rychard had sat down in the chair at the head of the table. One of the guards accompanying him had followed them into the room and was standing next to his liege Lord with an easy confidence, hands resting on the hilt of his sword. John looked up from examining the map to see them both watching him.

'Sit,' ordered Rychard, pointing at a chair. John obeyed, sitting bolt upright in the chair as if trying to sit to attention.

'So, what's your name, and what's so damned urgent?'

'John Cotterill my Lord. My, umm, boss came to see you earlier this afternoon.'

'Then why did you feel the need to come and pester me?' Rychard saw John hesitate. 'Out with it!'

'Begging your pardon, she didn't come back my Lord,' said John.

'She?' Rychard's demeanour perceptibly changed, becoming more intense. 'Describe her.'

'Blonde, blue eyes, a bit dangerous. Likes dressing in black. Goes by a different name every five minutes.'

'Hah!' Rychard appeared to be pleased with this description, 'My favourite spymaster,' his smile turned to a concerned frown, 'but you must be mistaken, she has not been to see me this afternoon.'

'She told me herself where she was going,' said John with a shrug.

'That does not bode well. However, you are here now, what news do you bring?'

John proceeded to share the tale of the trip to Hornbur and what they had discovered there, as well as Julienne's suspicions about a plot in Port Denly. After he had finished, Rychard stood, walked over to one of the windows and looked broodingly out into the city.

'This news is unwelcome, if not unexpected.' He was silent for a few moments before he turned back to face John. 'You spoke of a companion on your fact finding mission?'

'Yes, a dwarven shieldmaiden.'

'You also said the plotters are expecting a final delivery of powder. This and the name of the clan dwarves' contact, this Panely fellow, could be enough to convince the treacherous scum that your dwarven comrade is an agent of the clans bringing word of the shipment.'

'Yes my Lord.' John wasn't sure he liked the sound of this.

'So, what do you think of my plan?' Rychard turned to the guard as he asked this question.

John looked confused and was about to try and answer when the guard spoke, his voice strong and confident, 'A sound plan my Lord. Though a small modification may be in order.'

'This,' said Rychard, pointing at the sandy haired guard who had an impertinent grin on his face, 'is my chief spymaster, Luke. My plans are never good enough apparently. I'd have him flogged for his insolence, but he's almost always...' He stopped, glancing at Luke's raised eyebrow. 'Hah! I admit it, he's always right, damn it. So, what's wrong with it?'

'Trusting this commoner with so little proof.' Luke gestured at John.

John sat still, nervously listening to this exchange. He knew the lords of Asterland were not above a bit of torture to get confessions out of their enemies.

'Proof? He came to see us with this important intelligence. Isn't that proof enough of his loyalty?'

'My Lord, your trust in human nature does you credit. I, on the other hand, am paid to be despicable and untrusting. We should take steps to ensure this man is telling the truth and is, in fact, working for us.'

'See what I mean? Well, I dare say you're right. See to it will you.'

'Yes my Lord.' Luke gave a half bow to Rychard before waving his hand indicating that John should stand up. John did as he was bid, and was steered out of the room by Luke, a firm hand on his shoulder. Once outside Luke started talking as they walked. His grip relaxed, his hand resting companionably on John's shoulder.

'So, John. You're a loyal King's man then?'

'Yes, of course!' John sounded worriedly earnest.

'Your accent. You're from the east of the kingdom, one of the villages near the foothills of the Spiky mountains.' This was delivered as a statement, not a question.

'That's right,' said John, 'Highmill in Estershire.'

'Loyal Astish folk in Estershire, if a little simple.' Luke nodded at the guard as they walked out onto the balcony.

John opened his mouth to protest but stopped when he remembered what the people in his village were like, and his mouth snapped shut.

'And you John, are a prime example of a simpleton. No offence.' Luke continued his voice dropped to a near-whisper, 'strolling in, announcing you're an agent, the gods only know who's listening.'

'Ah,' said John, feeling every bit the simpleton as accused. They walked through a doorway and started down another stone clad corridor lit with flickering torches.

'My gut is telling me that you are who you say you are.'

John's relief was almost palpable.

'However, I regret to say that these matters cannot be left to my gut feeling.'

John's feeling of relief drained away, to be replaced by something he could only describe as 'cold dread'. By this time they had descended a spiral staircase and, by John's reckoning, were somewhere underneath the keep. Isn't that where the dungeons traditionally were?

Luke stopped by a stout wooden door, produced a key with a flourish and inserted it into the keyhole. He turned the key which produced a heavy metallic clunking noise. He pushed the door open, eliciting a melodramatic creak from the hinges, and indicated John should go through.

John hesitated, a pensive look on his face.

'I'm sorry, but I must insist.' Luke gave John a not so gentle shove into the room.

John stumbled as he crossed the threshold. His hand went to his sword as he recovered his balance and heard the door slam shut.

'Think again,' said Luke from behind him.

John turned and came face to face with a blade, held expertly in the chief spymaster's hand. He hadn't even heard it leave its scabbard. He slowly moved his hand away from his sword hilt, raising his hands, palms forward.

'Better,' said Luke approvingly, lowering his own weapon.

John looked around the room. It was lit by a guttering torch held in a bracket by the door. There were a number of chests against one wall, and some shelves were fixed to the rough stone walls above them. These shelves held various bottles and boxes labelled in a script he could not read. More worryingly, the shelves on the opposite wall held an array of painful looking torture implements and in the middle of the room was what looked like a rack. The kind people got stretched on, not the type you stored your toast in.

'Don't worry, this won't hurt.' Luke had moved to one of the less worrying shelves and picked up a glass bottle containing a dull green liquid. 'Here drink this.' He passed the bottle to a puzzled looking John.

'What is it?' John asked, turning the bottle around in his hands. The label was in a language John was unfamiliar with, written in a flowing cursive script.

'A little concoction that will help me determine if you are who you say you are. Now, please, take a seat and drink it.' Luke had pulled a wooden chair out from behind the torture equipment and placed it behind John.

Seeing little other option, he obeyed, lowering himself into the chair before pulling the stopper out of the bottle. The smell which wafted up into his nostrils was sweet and smelled faintly of strawberries. He looked up at Luke who was making drinking motions and nodding encouragingly. He shrugged and upended the contents of the bottle into his mouth. It actually tastes of strawberries, he thought as he swallowed the mixture.

CHAPTER 10

'Now close your eyes and relax, just listen to the sound of my voice.' Luke's voice was soft and even toned. 'You are feeling relaxed, I'm now counting backwards,' and he started to count, slow and measured, 'ten… nine… eight… seven…'

During this countdown, John felt his body start to tingle and go numb. His head lolled forwards, his chin resting on his chest.

'Six… five… four…' Luke's voice was distant, sounding as if it was at the end of a long tunnel.

'Three...two…one.'

The voice faded out as it counted down, replaced by the sound of his own heartbeat, slow and steady. John felt like he was floating, filled with a dreamy sense of well-being. His eyes were closed, and he was thinking of precisely nothing.

A faint, disembodied voice impinged on his blissful emptiness. 'John, I want you to tell me when you were hired. Think back.'

Dreamily John complied and reached back through his

memory; a small village square came into focus around him. He grew up here, Highmill.

'As agreed Twelve shillings.'

John watched the man count out twelve silver coins. His first bounty and vindication of his choice. Farming was for losers.

'Thank you, sir.' John took the coins, a broad smile on his face.

'We won't be losing any more sheep to that ne'er do well, you've done us a service.'

'Glad to have been of help,' said John, shaking the man's hand. 'I'd best be going before the light fails,' he said squinting up at the sky, noting the sun's position as it dipped behind the peaks of the Spiky mountains.

'All very interesting, but too far back. Tell me about your most recent job,' the disembodied voice echoed around him.

The village square became insubstantial, the buildings smearing across his vision, blurring together into a wood and brick coloured band. It all swirled around him for a few moments before slowing and resolving into an alleyway. He looked to his left and saw Bienia waving her sword at an athletic blonde woman lying on the ground who was wearing black, body-hugging clothes. Ah, Julienne, he thought. How had he forgotten that? She'd only just told them her name.

'Because he is a lying, traitorous weasel of a man, who knows I'm on to him,' said Julienne.

'What do you mean, on to him?' asked John.

'This is more like it,' the disembodied voice said. This time reality stayed put, and the scene played out exactly as before. John and Bienia ending up enlisting with Julienne, becoming agents for the King.

John opened his eyes to a finger click, disoriented. He was back in the room with the torture equipment.

Luke was standing in front of him. 'Welcome back, happy to say my gut feeling was correct,' he said smiling. 'Unhappily, your gut feeling is going to get somewhat, ah, looser. There's a bucket in the corner you can use.'

John looked at him and then at the indicated bucket, confused for a moment before he started to feel an urgent pressure in his belly. With a panicked look on his face, he lurched to his feet, and half ran, half hobbled to the bucket as he struggled to get his britches down before he ruined them. Luke looked away as John squatted down and noisily filled the bucket.

'I'm sorry, a regrettable side effect of the potion,' said Luke as he passed the unfortunate a damp rag. John used it to clean himself in an embarrassed silence, feeling wretched and empty.

Luke pulled some homespun woollen clothes from one of the chests and continued talking as he changed his clothes, replacing the armour and surcoat with the simple commoner's garb. 'I pity the cleaning staff really. Though a bucket of shit is one of the more innocuous things that needs cleaning up in this particular room.' He looked significantly at the rack in the middle of the room. Several dark stains were visible, splashed across its surface and the floor beneath it. He then swapped his sword for a small dagger, which he tucked into a boot.

Once John had finished wiping, Luke took a torch from the wall and led him down a dank, unlit stone passageway. This ran for fifty feet or so before ending at a flight of stone steps leading back up to ground level. At the top, they came to a wooden door. Luke slid a small wooden cover to one side, revealing a spyhole, and looked through. Apparently satisfied, he produced a key and unlocked the door, pulling it inwards to open it. John was surprised to see what appeared to be a bookcase on the back of the door.

'Can't go walking out of the front gate where just anyone can see us,' said Luke, 'this entrance is known only to loyal King's men, so keep it to yourself.'

On the other side of the bookcase door was a small, nondescript study. The window shutters were open a crack and John could make out the keep. They were in one of the houses overlooking the square he had left Bienia in earlier. There seemed to be a small crowd of people clustered around the fountain.

'We need to meet with your dwarven colleague, where is she?' Luke asked as he closed the door behind them.

John opened the shutters fully and pointed towards the fountain. 'Over there, I can't see her though, too many people in the way.'

'I see. Where are you all staying?'

'At an inn...' John looked at the ceiling as he struggled to remember the name. 'The Spread Eagle I think.'

This was met with a wry chuckle. 'She is nothing if not bold. Well, we can't go there to talk, we'll find somewhere else.'

'Why not?'

'That particular inn is a meeting place for Alliance agents.'

'Then why not shut it down?' asked John.

'We may know about them, but they do not know we

know. Therefore it is more useful to leave it and watch who comes and goes, obviously,' said Luke.

John wasn't really sure it was that obvious, but let it slide. 'Shall we go and find Bienia?'

Luke nodded his head towards the door, 'Of course. Please, lead on.'

He let John take the lead after they exited the house and walked over to the fountain. Once there, it became apparent what was holding the crowd's attention. Bienia had three of her playing cards laid out on the fountain's lip face down and was swapping them with each other in an apparently random fashion. There was a neatly dressed man standing next to the fountain tracking the movements of the cards intently. Bienia stopped switching the cards, making the last card swap with a flourish, 'Now then sir, to win the penny, where's the lady?'

The man pointed triumphantly at the card in the middle. Bienia flipped it over to reveal a seven of swords, said, 'Bad luck, it was here,' and flipped over the card to the left which revealed the queen.

'What? I was sure…' the man tailed off, looking confused.

Spotting John's disapproving face in the crowd, Bienia swiftly collected her cards.

'That's all I have time for folks,' she said as she pushed her way through the crowd towards him.

John grabbed her by the arm, dragging her out of the dispersing knot of people.

'You just can't help yourself can you?' he said.

'I got bored. Thought I'd raise a little beer money, no harm done,' Bienia protested, shrugging her arm out of his grip.

Luke looked on, a bemused look on his face. 'Come on you two, let's find somewhere a little less public to talk.'

Bienia looked him up and down. 'Who's this?'

'As far as I can make out, this is Julienne's boss,' said John.

'Which makes me your boss,' said Luke pointedly, 'so stop standing around chatting and follow me.'

Bienia looked from Luke to John and back again, shrugged and said, 'Lead on then… boss.'

He led them to a nearby inn which had been patriotically named The King's Arms. Having secured a table in a private booth and some drinks, Luke looked serious as he began to talk.

'John has briefed me on the situation, and now we must turn our attention to the detail of my Lord's plan.'

'Plan?' said Bienia, this would be a first as far as she was concerned.

'We intend to have you pose as a representative of the dwarves that sold the blasting powder and find out what it is going to be used for,' said Luke.

'Right,' said Bienia slowly, leaning back in her seat.

'What about Julienne?' asked John.

'Ah yes, the redoubtable Julienne.' Luke looked into his tankard as he swirled his ale around, then put it down and said 'I will endeavour to discover what has befallen her, while you two put my Lord's plan into effect.'

'Why don't you come with us?' Bienia asked.

'This is an important mission I am sending you on. As my lords chief spymaster, I will be preparing for a lack of success.' He smiled. 'I'm sure you understand that all eventualities must be planned for.'

'Right. Lack of success,' said John, his feeling of dread returning.

'All sounds a bit risky to me.' Bienia sounded sceptical.

'Of course, hazard pay will apply,' said Luke.

'It's funny, Julienne offered us the same when we went to Hornbur. Not seen any yet,' said Bienia. Her raised eyebrow invoiced Luke for work done.

Luke nodded and produced a leather money pouch, which he tossed in front of Bienia.

'That should cover your back pay, along with an advance for this next mission.'

Bienia picked up the pouch, hefted it experimentally and judged the weight to be acceptable. Glancing at John, she said, 'I'll look after this for now, we'll split it later,' and pocketed the pouch.

'Now that the account has been settled, may I continue with your instructions?' Luke asked in a reasonable tone.

'We're all square. Go for it,' said Bienia.

'You'll probably have already met your Alliance contact —' Luke began.

'We've stopped calling them NAFF now?' Bienia interrupted.

'They refer to themselves as the Alliance. NAFF is a somewhat derogatory acronym used by some of our agents. I don't really approve, as using it at the wrong time would be a bit of a giveaway.'

John leant forward and interrupted the interruption. 'Never mind that, who is this contact we've already met?'

'The innkeeper of the Spread Eagle. Leo.'

'Leo?' queried Bienia.

'Oh right,' said John, realisation dawning, 'makes sense, the Spread Eagle is a NAFF meeting place.'

'It is?' said Bienia, looking a little bewildered.

'Yes it is, and please stop saying NAFF,' said Luke.

'Sorry,' said John.

'Thank you,' said Luke. 'You'll tell him that you are from Hornbur and need to speak urgently with Derek Panely about the final shipment. It's unlikely that he has made it back to the city just yet so Leo will have to pass you up their chain of command.'

'What do we do when we're there?' asked John.

'As I said, we need you to find out what they are up to and report back. Oh and one more thing, you need to keep a low profile. No more marching in the front door of the keep declaring you are an agent of the King.'

'Why not? They're all King's men there, surely,' said Bienia.

Luke sighed heavily. 'That's the problem with the North. Most of the ungrateful buggers resent the redistribution of power that came with King Stephen's coronation. Makes it hard to know which ones to trust.'

'Pissed a few people off did he?' asked Bienia.

Luke laughed. 'That's one way of putting it. For some reason, they preferred it when the Denlys ran the show. Which means you need to be sure of who you talk to.'

'So how do we contact you when we have the information?' John asked.

'I will be in the house with the secret entrance for half an hour at midday each day. Meet me there when you are done.' Luke put his hands on the table, palms down. 'Be under no illusion, the mission you are undertaking is of the utmost importance. This plot is a danger to Asterland and must be stopped.'

'That much blasting powder could cause massive

destruction,' said Bienia. 'It would be a shame to see such a grand city damaged.'

'People could get hurt as well,' John added. Being overly concerned about architecture must be a dwarven thing, he thought.

'Then we have an accord.' Luke rose to his feet as he spoke. 'I look forward to your debriefing. Good luck.' With that, he pulled his hood up and exited the inn.

As John watched him go, Bienia picked up Luke's abandoned tankard. 'Do you think he doesn't want this then?' she asked, not waiting for an answer as she tipped the contents into her tankard, topping up her drink.

'I'd say not,' said John absently, deep in thought as he considered what they had been asked to do.

Bienia took a long drink of ale before disturbing his train of thought. 'We're most definitely spies now. There's a career change I wasn't expecting.'

'At least we're on the right side, for King and country and all that.'

'For the good of Asterland eh? Not even my bloody country.'

'You're being well paid,' John pointed out.

Bienia brightened at this reminder. 'Yes I am, aren't I?'

She drained her tankard, hopped down from the bench seat, gestured towards the door and said, 'Well, we'd better make sure they get their money's worth. Coming?'

CHAPTER 11

The Spread Eagle was relatively quiet by the time they returned. The lunchtime rush had abated and the evening trade was a couple of hours away from picking up. There were a handful of afternoon regulars at the bar, leaving them the pick of the empty tables. Leo was clearing and wiping tables, working his way methodically along the length of the room. John and Bienia sat at a table which was still cluttered with plates and empty tankards and waited for the innkeeper to come and clear it.

Sure enough, Leo hurried over to their table and started clearing the dirty crockery.

'What can I get you two?' he asked.

'Two ales,' said Bienia, 'and a meeting with the Alliance.'

Leo almost dropped the stack of plates he was carrying. 'The Alliance? What's that then?'

John noticed a bead of sweat forming on Leo's brow.

Bienia continued, ignoring the question. 'I have news about a certain shipment they are expecting.'

'Shipment? I'm sorry miss, I don't know what you're talking about.'

'I need to talk to Derek Panely. About the shipment from Hornbur,' said Bienia.

'Shhh, keep it down.' Leo glanced at the regulars sitting at the bar nursing their ales.

Bienia lowered her voice. 'It's important that I see Mister Panely. Now.'

Leo hesitated before he replied, 'Follow me.'

He waited for them to stand up, casting quick glances over his shoulder, before leading them through a door behind the bar. It opened into the kitchen; sausages and haunches of salted meat were hanging from hooks against one wall, and a fire was burning in a fireplace. A short, skinny woman with mousy brown hair tied into a bun was washing plates, pots and pans in a stone sink. She looked up questioningly as they entered.

'Alliance business Lily. Shut the door after us,' said Leo as he dumped the plates next to the sink.

Lily nodded wordlessly and went back to cleaning the now slightly larger mound of dirty crockery.

Leo moved to an iron-bound wooden trapdoor set into the floor. He lifted it open using the attached iron ring to reveal a set of wooden steps leading down into darkness.

A battered brass lantern and an equally well-used tinderbox rested on top of a wooden crate next to the now open trapdoor.

Leo lit the lantern with well-practised ease and beckoned them to follow as he descended the wooden steps.

At the bottom of the steps, they found themselves in a damp cellar. Barrels of ale and foodstuffs were stacked untidily around them. Ignoring most of the cellar's contents, Leo led them to a particularly dark corner which contained a stack of ale barrels. Leo grunted as he lifted the barrels one by one, moving them to one side. This slowly revealed an arched opening in the wall. The brickwork surrounding it was clearly newer than the rest of the cellar. Peering through the archway, they could see a rough cut passage through the earth, wooden support beams placed at regular intervals to keep the ceiling from collapsing.

'This way,' said Leo.

They followed the innkeeper through the archway. John and Leo had to stoop to avoid bashing their heads on the wooden beams. Bienia, on the other hand, found she had plenty of headroom.

Leo started talking as they progressed along the passage which gently sloped downwards, the earthen walls giving way to rough cut stone.

'Derek's not in Port Denly at the moment,' said Leo, 'so I'm taking you to see Simon. Things are pretty hectic right now; the last thing we need is a screw up with the blasting powder.'

'Simon, right.' Bienia wasn't sure if she was supposed to know who this was.

'Simon Denly. The son of old Lord Denly,' said Leo. 'We're going to restore him as Lord here, get rid of that southern swine, Mayhew.'

'Good, good, he'll want to hear what I have to say.'

John was wondering what it was she was going to say. They really should have discussed this before approaching Leo. As they continued on their underground journey, John thought he could hear the rush of running water over stone.

'Right, mind your step,' said Leo. 'This bit can be slippery.'

The noise of running water grew louder until the passageway opened up into a natural cave which was around fifty feet across. A wooden bridge spanned the fast flowing water of an underground river. The wood of the bridge glistened, slick with water spray. A rope stretched across one side of the bridge served as a handrail of sorts.

Leo led the way across, Bienia and John carefully keeping one hand on the rope at all times as they followed. On the other side was the entrance to another man-made passageway similar to the first. Without hesitation, Leo took them into it, ducking slightly into the low entrance. This passage did not lead downwards, but ran straight for fifty feet or so and ended in a round iron plate. There were hinges on one side, suggesting it could be opened.

'Ugh, smells like an army camp latrine,' said Bienia.

Leo put his lantern down next to a large clay pot. Just above the pot, there was a hook fixed to the wall which had several long strips of cloth draped over it. Leo took one, lifted the lid of the pot and dipped a strip in the liquid it contained. He then wrung it out before tying it so that it covered his nose and mouth. He motioned for John and Bienia to do the same. They did not need much persuasion and quickly followed suit, tying the strips of cloth dipped in perfumed oil in place. This gave them considerable relief from the noxious smell filling this part of the passage.

'Welcome to the city sewer,' said Leo as he pushed the plate open on its rusted iron hinges. It clanged against the wall noisily. The echoing sound of iron on stone gave way to the murmur of gently running water. This was accompanied by a redoubling of the disgusting smell which was, thankfully, somewhat ameliorated by the primitive perfumed face masks they wore.

Leo stepped through the opening, turned and gestured for them to follow. Somewhat reluctantly they did, stepping onto a narrow brick walkway next to a flowing river of excrement. The sewer walls were made of brick and covered in a sheen of damp, slimy liquid. By the light of Leo's lantern, they could see solid objects floating past on the, for want of a better word, water.

'This day just keeps getting better,' said John.

Leo smiled as he heaved the plate closed, sealing them in the sewer.

'I don't come down here unless I have to. Which I think is the point. We're not going to get visits from King's agents down here.'

'Of course,' said John, with a nod.

'Well, let's not stand around here discussing the merits of a sewer hideout, follow me!'

Leo led them down the sewer tunnels. When a choice of ways faced them, John noticed the way was marked with a crude 'X' scratched into the wall. He was beginning to wonder if they were being led in circles when Leo stopped at another iron plate mounted in the wall. This was also marked with an 'X'.

'Here we are,' said Leo as he pulled the heavy iron plate open. The hinges groaned as he did so, echoing around the sewer.

They climbed through into one end of a narrow stone clad passageway. John noted a similar set of perfume and rags on a hook as they had found at the other end of their trip. Leo pulled the plate shut before removing his rag mask. John and Bienia followed suit, draping the rags over the hook. Once they had done this, Leo squeezed past them and led them onward down the passage towards a meeting with Simon Denly.

CHAPTER 12

At the end of the passage was a sturdy wooden door. They were now far enough away from the sewer entrance that the smell had faded, the slime on their boots and a vague whiff of something unsavoury the only lingering sign of their trip. Leo carefully rapped out a series of knocks on the door and then stood, waiting patiently. His patience was soon rewarded, the door opened by a large man who was holding a sword at the ready.

'Hello, Leo. Sorry about the sword, can't be too careful,' he said as he sheathed the sword in the scabbard at his waist.

'Got a visitor from the Silver Hills to see Simon.' Leo indicated Bienia, who gave a little wave.

'Right.' He looked surprised, pausing for a moment before he nodded and moved aside, motioning them through. Once they were all the other side of the door, he pushed it shut and lifted a heavy bar into position, securing it.

They had entered a small torchlit room containing a chair and a table. On the table was a half eaten pie on a battered pewter plate. They'd clearly interrupted the man's dinner.

'Ok you two, give me your weapons,' said the man in a no-nonsense tone. 'Don't worry you'll get them back,' he added when he saw their hesitation.

John and Bienia handed their swords over. Bienia kept her shield on her back which seemed to not count as a weapon as far as their host was concerned.

'Been a busy day Leo. Dave brought in a King's spy this morning. We got a tip-off from the Stonebridge crew,' said the man conversationally as he put the swords on the table next to his pie.

'A spy?' Leo asked.

'Yeah, apparently killed the watch captain. He was one of ours.'

Bienia moved closer to John and whispered, 'Julienne.'

John wanted to ask what they had done with the spy, but restrained himself, forcing himself to look unconcerned. Fortunately, he did not need to contain himself for long as the man led them down another passage, soon reaching another door.

'Stay here for a second, let me tell Simon you're here,' said the man.

He left the three of them outside the door while he went to do just that. They heard muffled voices from the other side of the door before it was reopened and they were ushered into a bare room containing a chair, a cluttered writing table and a simple sleeping pallet. A lantern rested on the writing table throwing long shadows on the wall behind them.

'What message is it that you have for me?'

The speaker was standing next to the writing table, a

fair-haired man of average build, wearing functional, comfortable clothes. This was Simon Denly, who, if Leo was to be believed, was the rightful Lord of Port Denly and the surrounding lands.

'My name is Bienia of the Ironfist clan, daughter of Briggi, grand-daughter of Shugga, shieldmaiden of the clans of the Silver Hills,' said Bienia, her voice strong and clear.

'All very impressive I'm sure, but what message do you bring?'

'I bring news from the commander of Hornbur,' said Bienia. 'The last shipment of powder will be a few days late.'

'What? Why? Are you sure? How do I know you are who you say you are?'

'Which question would you like me to answer first?'

'I think I will satisfy myself on the last question first,' said Simon. He opened a box that was on the writing table and pulled out a small glass bottle containing a dull green liquid which looked suspiciously familiar to John.

'Now, unfortunately, this' – Simon held the bottle in front of him – 'does not work on dwarven physiology. Fortunately, you have a companion who it will work on. Leo, go and get a bucket and a damp cloth.'

John watched Leo leave the room on his errand and felt a growing sense of alarm. It was the same potion as Luke had used on him. A disaster on two counts. First, he was about to get flushed out again, and he didn't think he had much left to give. Second, if Simon asked the wrong question their ruse would be uncovered.

'You can trust me, I work for Captain Marrian in Stonebridge,' said John. It was the best he could do. If he could get Simon to ask the right question this might turn out only to be a disaster on the first count.

'Do you now? Well, we'll soon see about that. Sit there, drink this.' Simon pointed at the chair and held out the bottle.

John took the bottle and sat down as he was asked. Then he hesitated, looking in dread at the mixture.

'Now please,' said Simon.

Mentally bracing himself for what was about to happen, he drank the familiar strawberry tasting liquid. Yes, no doubt about it, this was the same stuff. His feeling of nervous anticipation was damped as he felt the concoction start to take hold.

Bienia watched, bemused, as Simon counted John down into a trance. John's head thumped forward on the count of zero.

'Tell me about your employment with Captain Marrian,' Simon asked the now gently drooling John.

John proceeded to murmur out a detailed account of his first meeting with Captain Marrian, complete with a description of the poster advertising a used cart for sale. This seemed to satisfy Simon, who clicked his fingers. John's head snapped upright, and his eyes slowly regained focus.

By this point, Leo had returned with a bucket. Wordlessly he placed it down next to John.

'Probably best you leave for this bit,' Leo suggested to Bienia.

'Why? What's going to happen?'

She then heard a wet splat and John groaning behind her as he squatted over the bucket.

'Ah, I see,' she said and hastily exited the room with

Simon, leaving John to finish his movement and clean himself up under the vigilant eyes of Leo and the other man.

Bienia took this opportunity to be a good spy and try to find something out. 'So, what are you using the powder for?'

'We're going to blow up the King and his cursed cousin Lord Mayhew,' said Simon grimly, 'I just hope what we have is enough.'

'Why not just wait until you have it all?'

'The King isn't visiting Port Denly for long, we need to strike while he is here with Mayhew. Once they are out of the way, I will assume control of Port Denly as is my birthright.'

At this point, Bienia realised Simon quite liked the sound of his own voice and didn't need much encouragement to talk about his plans.

'Aren't you worried about how the southern Lords will react?'

'No, with the military assistance from your High King they won't be able to do a thing.' He paused before asking in a slightly suspicious tone, 'don't you know about that already?'

'Oh yes, of course,' said Bienia, inwardly cursing as she tried to cover up her blunder. 'I'm glad you realise how good dwarven soldiers are.'

'Your High King's offer of help is greatly appreciated. When my lands are restored, and the new republic of Asterland formed he will reap the rewards for his assistance.'

Bienia wasn't sure she knew what a republic was or what help the High King could give, seeing as the post was mostly ceremonial, but she knew it was probably not good news for the current King of Asterland. Not good news. That reminded her. Worry about the High King later; it was time to see if Julienne was still alive.

'What about this spy you captured?' she asked.

'She is being questioned as we speak.'

'Are you using one of those potions?'

'No. They are hard to obtain. Also, you need to know what questions to ask. A good, old-fashioned interrogation is more effective in these situations,' said Simon.

'Right.' She had a feeling that 'good' and 'old fashioned' in this context probably meant torture.

'Your companion will be a few minutes cleaning up, come and watch with me.'

Bienia followed him back to the first room and down another stone clad passage. She wondered when and why this underground complex had been built. It can't have always been a hideout. Her wandering thoughts were interrupted when they arrived at their destination.

Bienia's eyes were drawn to a woman dressed in black, hanging by her arms in the middle of the room. Her head was bowed, and her blonde hair hung down over her face. The heavy manacles on her wrists were connected to a chain looped over a hook in the ceiling.

A man stood to one side perusing a table of iron implements designed for inflicting pain. The torturer, Bienia presumed. A second man was standing to the side, next to the door they had just entered. He acknowledged the two new arrivals with a nod and a slight look of surprise at the presence of a dwarf in their hideout.

'Have we missed much?' asked Simon.

'Not really. Just the initial beating,' said the torturer.

'Has she said anything yet?' asked Bienia.

Hearing a dwarven accent, the woman's head raised slightly, and Bienia got a look at her face, confirming her identity and the initial beating. Julienne's face was a bit of a mess. A particularly nasty cut above her eye was dripping blood down the side of her face and onto the floor. Bienia saw a slight smile as their eyes briefly met before Julienne dropped her head again.

'Not yet,' said the torturer. He selected a steel poker, shoving the tip into a brazier, nestling it into some glowing coals.

'Where are you going to burn her?' Simon asked.

'Inside thigh to start with,' said the man. He sounded like he was discussing the day's grocery shopping, his tone disinterested.

'Oh good,' said Simon. His tone was one of extreme interest.

His eagerness unsettled Bienia. She understood that torture had its place in the repertoire of the professional interrogator, but that didn't mean he had to enjoy it.

'I think I've seen enough,' said Bienia.

'Really? He's just getting warmed up.' Simon pointed at the steel poker, chuckling at his own pun.

'Yes. If you don't mind, I'll pick up my friend and ask Leo to take us back.'

'Of course. Thank you for delivering your message Bienia Ironfist.' Simon turned to the man by the door. 'Jenkins, take our guest back to my office, then come back. We'll give this another hour before we finish for the day.'

Soon Bienia and John were reunited and making their way back through the sewer, guided by Leo. Both John and Leo said nothing the whole journey back. Bienia presumed this was in joint embarrassment about John's forced bowel movement. She was content to walk in silence; worry about the involvement of her people, the clans of the Silver Hills, weighing on her mind.

CHAPTER 13

John had snuffed the lantern out an hour ago. Moonlight bathed his inn room in a gentle light, revealing him sitting on the bed, still dressed in his leather armour with his sword belt on. He was full of nervous energy and wanted to get on with rescuing Julienne. After he had been waiting for what seemed like half the night, he finally heard the quiet tap on the door that he had been waiting for. Opening the door, he stepped out onto the landing and then carefully shut it behind him, trying to minimise any noise.

'Ready?' whispered Bienia.

'Yes, let's go.'

They slowly made their way along the landing and down the stairs into the common room. The occasional clank of Bienia's armour sounded overly loud to John's ears, but no-one seemed to be woken by it.

Their plan was simple. Retrace their steps in the sewer by following the scratched 'X' symbols they had followed with Leo and use the secret knock to gain entrance to the hideout. Then subdue the guard on the door, get to the torture room and, finally, rescue Julienne.

They executed the first part flawlessly. John even

remembered the pattern of knocking first time. The guard's confusion at seeing them again gave them the opening they needed to overpower and tie him up. It wasn't until they got to the torture room that the plan failed them. Sure enough, Julienne was still there. She was alone, lying in the corner of the room, still wearing the manacles with the connecting chain pooled beside her head. Another chain had one end fixed to a ring cemented into the wall, the other shackled to her leg. A shackle. They both looked at it. A shackle that needed a key.

'Shit,' said John.

Bienia looked around the room, her eyes lighting upon the table full of torture implements.

'We can use some of these tools to free her,' she said. 'Wake her up.'

While Bienia inspected the tools at their disposal, John moved to Julienne. He frowned at the sight of her swollen, battered face and her raw, weeping burns which were visible where her leggings had been torn away. He grabbed her shoulders, intending to shake her awake.

'I'm not asleep, pain's been keeping me awake.'

'Good. I mean, sorry. For the pain I mean,' said John, glancing at the burns on her inside thigh.

'Up here.' She smiled weakly. 'I appreciate the sentiment. Was wondering when the cavalry would show up.'

'We're here now. Do you think you can walk?'

'Yes. Fortunately, they haven't got round to breaking any bones in my legs yet. I'm going to be sod all use in a sword fight though.' She nodded at her right hand. John could see two of the fingers looked broken.

'Here we go.' Bienia had a hammer and chisel in her hand. 'Let's have a crack at this chain then.'

After inspecting the shackles and chain, she moved to the metal ring cemented into the wall. Nodding to herself she set the chisel against the cement and brought the hammer down with a sharp crack.

'I'll keep an eye down the passage,' said John.

A few more well-placed blows and Bienia could pull the chain from the wall. 'I'm afraid you'll have to carry the chains with you until we can get to a locksmith.'

'I'll manage,' said Julienne, getting to her feet.

She was gathering the chains into her arms when John said, 'There's someone coming, quick, back on the floor. Bee?'

He motioned for Bienia to join him by the doorway. She hastily made her way over, and they both flattened themselves against the wall while Julienne lay back on the floor, feigning sleep. Listening, they could hear the steady tread of someone approaching. Bienia nodded at John who lifted his sword in readiness.

As the man entered the room, they could see it was the torturer.

'What's all this noise then? Are you ready for some more fun little girl?' His tone was cruel.

Julienne raised her head and looked at him, smiling through her split, blood-caked lips. 'Are you?'

Before he could answer John brought the pommel of his sword down hard onto the back of his head, and he crumpled to the floor.

'I don't suppose he has some keys?' Julienne asked as she hefted what felt like a hundred weight of chains she was expected to carry.

Bienia knelt and plucked a keyring from the unconscious man's belt. 'You're in luck.'

Julienne was soon freed from her restraints and, with John's help, transferred the shackles to her torturer and hung him from the hook in the ceiling. She couldn't resist giving him a punch in the groin before they left the room, leaving him gently spinning, chains rattling.

They hurried down the passage and into the entry room where they had left the door guard gagged and tied up.

Julienne looked at the hogtied man and said to Bienia, 'Nice rope work, yours?'

'Not me, John.'

Julienne nodded approvingly at John and then asked, 'Did he get a look at you before you knocked him out?'

'Yes, I think so,' said John.

'Then kill him.'

'What? He's tied up, we don't need to,' said John.

'He's seen you. Your cover will be compromised if you let him live. No witnesses.'

'She's right,' said Bienia. 'I don't like ending a man outside of a fight, but we have to John.'

'It's always your first answer, like that poor woodcutter. You were ready to murder him too.' John was visibly upset.

'Colin,' said Julienne, 'and I'll admit that wasn't necessary as it turned out. This, however, is. So get on with it, we don't have time to waste.'

John just stood there in silence.

'If that's a problem for you, I'll do it. Just give me a blade'. Julienne extended her uninjured hand.

'Can't we take him with us? Arrest him?' John asked, already knowing the answer.

'I don't fancy our chances of making a speedy getaway carrying him, do you?'

John was conflicted, he really didn't like the idea of killing this man. However, Julienne was right. If they left him here, the Alliance would soon know of his and Bienia's involvement in Julienne's escape, and their life expectancy would shorten dramatically.

'Alright. I'll do it,' he said quietly.

Julienne dropped her outstretched arm and stared at him for a moment before nodding and turning away.

John drew his sword and knelt next to the man. He knew this needed to be done, but he didn't feel good about it. He remained motionless for a few seconds, whispered, 'I'm sorry,' and then cut through the man's carotid artery. He watched, an anguished look on his face, as the man's life blood pulsed out onto the floor.

'Come on. There's nothing more to do here,' said Bienia, resting her hand on John's shoulder.

Nodding, he wiped his sword on his victim's jerkin and stood up. There was a slight tremor in his voice as he said, 'Let's get moving.'

They soon arrived at the iron plate leading to the sewer. Julienne wrinkled her nose in disgust. 'What is that smell?'

'Forgot to mention, we're leaving through the sewer,' said Bienia as she fixed a perfumed rag in place.

'I'd like to say you get used to it, but, well, you don't,' said John, handing her one of the rags.

'Thanks,' said Julienne, and hurriedly fixed her mask in place. With that done, the trio started the unpleasant trek back to the inn, talking in muffled voices as they splashed their way through the sewer.

'What's the plan once we're out of here?' Julienne asked.

'We hole up in our rooms until tomorrow, then go and meet Luke,' said John.

'Is that wise? What if Leo sees me?'

'We'll keep you in my room,' said Bienia, 'he's not going to disturb an agent of Hornbur.'

Julienne nodded, 'Even if he does see me, he may not make the connection between the captured spy and me. After all, Lucinda has never been to Stonebridge.'

'Lucinda?' John asked and then thought back to talking with Leo at breakfast, 'Oh right, that's the name he knows you by.'

'That's alright, I sometimes have trouble keeping track myself,' said Julienne, patting John on the shoulder. Her eyes twinkled, hinting at a smile hidden behind the mask.

The trip back to the inn was uneventful, except for a tense moment when Julienne stumbled in the kitchen as she climbed out of the trapdoor and knocked an iron pot onto the floor. The three of them froze as the metallic clatter of the pot on the stone flagstones filled the night with noise. However, after a tense minute had passed it became clear that no-one had been woken and breathing a sigh of relief, they made it to their rooms without further mishap. John whispered good night to the two women before heading to his room, and Julienne gratefully collapsed onto the bed in Bienia's room.

'Right, now to sort those fingers out,' said Bienia.

Julienne looked at her right hand glumly. 'This is going to hurt, isn't it?'

'Yes, so bite down on this.' Bienia passed her a wooden spoon.

'A spoon?'

'Best I could come up with on short notice.'

Julienne took the proffered spoon, put it in her mouth and closed her eyes, holding out her injured hand. She felt Bienia take hold of her fingers and pull. She bit down hard on the spoon as excruciating pain washed over her. After Bienia had reset the fingers to her satisfaction, she snapped the spoon in half to use as a makeshift splint. Once she had finished her ministrations, Julienne fell back with a thump onto the bed, swiftly falling into a deep sleep despite the throbbing of her fingers and the painful burns on her inside thighs. Bienia stripped out of her armour and using her rolled up rain cloak as a pillow, settled down to sleep on the floor.

When Julienne woke, the dwarf was gone. She lay stretched out on the bed, sunlight streaming through the window, the morning sky bright and free of clouds. The pain of her burns was still excruciating when she moved or accidentally brushed them with the bed clothes, so she lay as still as she could while she waited for the morning to slip round.

After what seemed like an eternity, a key rattled in the door before it opened to admit Bienia and John. John turned and took a quick look up and down the landing before shutting the door carefully behind them.

'Is it time?' Julienne asked.

'If we are going to go, we need to go now,' said John.

Bienia held out a dark green hooded cloak. 'We took a

trip to the market, to get you this. We're assuming that Denly is going to have his agents out looking for you.'

'Good thinking,' said Julienne, sitting up and swinging her legs out of the bed with a grimace. She was still dressed in her black outfit, bloodstains and ripped trousers included.

'How did they get you last time?' John asked.

'It was the watchmen at the keep gate. They had a picture of me and had me bundled away before I knew what was happening,' said Julienne as she put on the cloak. It came down to just above knee height, hiding the worst of her injuries and damaged clothes.

'Marrian must have sent the pictures before, well, you know,' said John.

'Stupid. I should have realised when you two showed up with a picture. It wasn't the only one. How do I look?' Julienne asked this as she shuffled around in an approximation of a twirl, the cloak wrapped around her.

'If you keep your head down, no-one would know you've been recently tortured,' said Bienia.

'Good enough, let's go,' said John.

They then left the room, descended the stairs, made it out of the inn without encountering Leo and lost themselves in the crowded city streets.

Either the cloak was doing its job, or no-one was looking for them, as their trip through the city passed without incident. They arrived at the house with the secret entrance to the keep just before noon. The door was unlocked, and they quickly slipped inside. John closed the door behind them and made sure the window shutters were closed against prying eyes. They then sat at the table to wait for the arrival of Luke.

'Beggar's Five anyone?' asked Bienia as she produced her deck of cards and started to shuffle them.

Julienne raised an eyebrow and was about to reply when there was a scraping noise as the bookcase swung open to reveal Luke, who looked somewhat surprised to see Julienne alive and well and about to be bilked by Bienia.

'Well, I didn't expect to find you here,' he said.

'Hello, chief,' said Julienne nonchalantly.

'It appears I may have underestimated you both,' said Luke with an approving nod at John and Bienia.

'We found her when we went to meet Simon Denly,' said John.

'Simon Denly? Do tell me more. And by more, I mean what his plans are for the explosive.'

'They're planning to blow up what's his name,' said Bienia.

'She means King Stephen,' explained Julienne, suppressing a laugh as it rippled pain along her bruised ribs.

'King Stephen, yes,' Bienia confirmed.

'Do you know where exactly they plan to carry out this perfidious deed?' Luke asked.

'All I know is that it will be in Port Denly somewhere.'

'Unfortunately, that doesn't help us find the powder that is already here,' said Luke. 'We do however have men watching the gates for the final shipment coming in from Stonebridge. Finding and following that should lead us to the rest of the infernal stuff.'

'Are you going to raid the sewer hideout?' John asked.

'For the moment, no. Until the King arrives, Lord Rychard's personal guard are the only ones we can trust, and they number only a dozen. I will order a raid if we have to, but I would rather not tip our hand.' Luke pointed at John and Bienia. 'You two return to the inn and maintain your cover. Spend some time pretending to be new to the city and wait to see if you are contacted again.'

'I think we can manage that,' said John.

'That's the spirit, go and enjoy spending some of that hazard pay. Let me worry about intercepting the final shipment of blasting powder.'

CHAPTER 14

They spent their time idling the days away in the Spread Eagle Inn, interspersed with sightseeing trips around the city. The sightseeing generally consisted of what Bienia called a 'pub crawl', which involved the pair of them trying to visit as many of the cities drinking establishments as they could until John admitted defeat and they weaved their way unsteadily back to the inn.

As the day of the King's arrival approached, it seemed the Alliance lost interest in them, and they saw less and less of Leo who was being kept busy with the influx of guests. There was an increase in visitors throughout the city, and anticipation of the event was starting to build. Bunting was being put up, musicians were practising, and plenty of drink and fine foodstuffs were being stockpiled by the cities various eating establishments.

After several days John was surprised to see that Bienia appeared to be becoming bored with drinking and gambling. Maybe it was the fact that the money was running out; their bar tab now exceeded Bienia's winnings by a considerable margin, eating into their hazard pay. There weren't many players of Beggar's Five who had not lost money to her as she dominated games throughout the cities gambling dens. As a result of this uncanny ability at cards, she was now not welcome at many tables, removing the money making opportunities of playing in high-stake games.

The morning of the King's arrival finally came. The pair headed down to the docks, where the royal ship would be arriving, in an attempt to snag a position with a good viewpoint. Bienia was carrying a pair of leather canteens, which she had filled with ale, slung over her shoulders. They made a pleasingly full sloshing sound as she walked.

The tall masts of ships rose above the rooftops as they got closer to the harbour. They joined a moderately sized crowd of people also walking in the direction of the sea, continuing along the cobbled street until they finally rounded a bend in the road and saw the dockside and a growing crowd of onlookers.

One of the piers that stretched out into the water was being kept clear of the general peasantry by several city watchmen. This, they surmised, was where the King's ship would dock. They threaded their way through the crowd along the dockside and eventually managed to find an unoccupied low wall near the waterfront to sit on.

'Drink?' There was a pop as Bienia uncorked one of the canteens of ale.

'A bit early for me,' said John.

Bienia took a long drink and wiped her mouth with the back of her hand. Then she wrinkled her nose and asked, 'What's that smell?'

There was a faint smell of sewage wafting around them, which may have explained why no-one had been sitting on the wall.

'I think there's a sewer outlet near here,' said John, waving in the direction of the water.

Bienia jumped down from the wall, gave an exuberant bow and said, 'We welcome you, King what's his name, don't mind the pong, that's just our shit.'

John laughed. 'It does seem a fine welcome to give your monarch doesn't it?'

She grinned back at him and turned to look at the growing crowd. 'I thought he wasn't that popular?'

'They just love a good show. And it's a good excuse to stuff your face with food and get drunk.'

'Always a good way to win people over. Speaking of stuffing your face, how about a meat pie?' She nodded towards a nearby trestle table, laden with pies, which was set back from the waterfront, away from the smell of the sewer outlet.

'Sure, I'll go get some.'

As John approached the pie seller, he recognised him as Leo.

'Two pies please Leo,' he asked.

'That'll be tuppence,' said Leo.

John fished out the coins from his money pouch and passed them to Leo. He noticed the man wasn't his usual chatty self and seemed to be sweating more than usual as he passed him the pies.

He returned with the meaty bounty and passed one of the pies to Bienia.

'Well, he looks nervous,' he said.

'Who?' Bienia asked and took a bite from the pie, chewing with obvious relish.

'Leo. He's here. Selling pies and looking nervous.'

Bienia mumbled around a mouthful of pastry and meat,

'Nervous? What's he got to be nervous about? This pie is delicious.'

'I don't think it's the pies he's nervous about,' said John.

Bienia swallowed her mouthful of pie. 'The blasting powder?'

'Yes, I think it's getting used today. The question is, where?' John looked around as if he might spot the explosive just lying around somewhere. 'Must be the docks somewhere. Why else would Leo be here looking nervous?'

'The sewer,' said Bienia. 'It empties out near here right? That's what that smell is.'

'The sewer?'

'Think about it, how do you move that much powder around the city without being seen?'

'Right, they're hiding out down there already. It makes sense.'

'Where have they put it? Not under there.' She gestured at the pier being kept clear for the King's arrival. 'Way too wet.'

'Why take it out of the sewer at all? It probably runs right under the docks.'

Bienia dropped the remains of her pie. 'Shit, that's why they needed so much, to make sure they collapse the entire harbourside.'

'We need to tell someone,' said John.

'Who?' Bienia asked. 'All those guards on the pier are Northerners. We don't know if we can trust them, remember what happened to Julienne?'

'We should find and tell Luke or one of Lord Rychards men.'

'I don't think we have time for that, look,' said Bienia. She pointed out to sea where a tall-masted ship, the wind billowing its sails, was rounding the headland to the south. It was bedecked with flags and streaming pennants.

'The King's ship?' asked John, a sinking feeling in his stomach.

'I'm guessing that's what all those flags and stuff are about.' She ran her hand over her cropped hair. 'Looks like it's up to us then, but what do we do?'

'We need to find out exactly where the powder is,' said John.

They both turned and looked at the pie stall and exclaimed simultaneously, 'Leo!'

Fortunately, Leo had not noticed their sudden interest and was just finishing serving a customer when the pair approached his table, splitting up so that they came at him one on each side. John coughed to get the man's attention.

Leo jumped perceptibly before he recognised them, 'Oh, you gave me a turn then.'

'Hello, Leo, we hope you can help us out,' said John.

'Help you out? What with?'

'We need to know where the blasting powder is.'

Leo's brow furrowed in confusion. 'Why would you want to know that?'

John saw the ship getting closer to the pier and grabbed the man roughly by the front of his shirt. 'We don't have time for this, tell us where the blasting powder is.'

'You've been paid, get off me!'

'Now there's where you've made a mistake. Just because I'm a dwarf.' Bienia shook her head in mock disapproval.

'A mistake?' Leo echoed, as he struggled to escape John's grip.

'You think all dwarves obey the High King. Well, we don't. I'm an Ironfist and a ruthless agent of your King what's his name, so you better start talking.' A short knife had appeared in Bienia's hand.

'What?' said Leo. He looked even more confused, though the sight of the knife seemed to have stopped him from trying to pull away from John's grip.

'King Stephen. She means King Stephen,' said John.

'That's right. So if you know what's good for you, you'll start talking.' Bienia made a mock stabbing motion with her knife.

At this point, Leo appeared to find some backbone and said, 'Never.' Then gave the game away when his eyes briefly darted down at an iron manhole cover under the table.

'Thanks, Leo,' said John, shifting his grip to Leo's arm. He pulled the arm up behind the man, eliciting a small cry of pain.

John took a quick look around. No-one seemed to have noticed the altercation with Leo. Even though this part of the dockside had a good view of the harbour, it was relatively empty due to the sewage smell permeating the area. This was also probably why Leo's stall was up here, rather than down amongst the crowd where he'd make more pie sales.

'Open it,' he told Leo, shoving him towards the manhole cover as he released his arm.

Leo cast a nervous glance at the knife being held by Bienia and then acquiesced, bending down and lifting the cover, moving it to one side. The rank smell of the sewer intensified, and John momentarily wished for the perfumed rag masks they wore on their last sojourn below the city streets.

A voice floated up out of the darkness, 'Is it time then?'

Leo never got a chance to answer as Bienia's boot connected with his backside sending him falling down the hole. There was a thump, a splash and a curse as Leo fell on top of whoever was down there. Bienia then jumped into the hole, landing on the two men in a clatter of armour. A scream of pain echoed around the sewer, followed by more cursing.

John, however, took a more considered approach. Having discovered the iron rungs of a ladder, he descended into the sewer in a more controlled fashion, stepping off of the bottom rung onto a narrow walkway next to Bienia and the two alliance conspirators. They were lit by the pale glow of a lantern which was precariously placed on the edge of the walkway but had somehow managed to escape being knocked into the flowing sewage.

'Everything under control?' he asked.

'Apart from wanting to throw up because of the smell? Yes,' said Bienia from her position on top of the two men.

'No,' said Leo. The back of his head was resting in the 'lumpy water' flowing down the centre of the sewer. His arms were being pinned by Bienia, who was sitting on him and using her weight to keep Leo and the man below him in place. This may not have been totally necessary, as the unfortunate on the bottom of the pile was not moving and appeared to have been knocked out by one of the impacts from above.

'I think my leg's broken,' said Leo plaintively.

Bienia looked over her shoulder at his left leg, which was bent at an unnatural angle.

'I think you're right. Now, which way to the blasting powder?'

'I'm not telling you that.'

Bienia got to her feet, accidentally stepping on the injured leg as she did so, eliciting a howl of pain from Leo. She stood looking at the leg thoughtfully for a moment while Leo laced the air with some creative swearing.

'Sorry, what was that? I couldn't hear over all the screaming.' She lifted her booted foot, holding it over his leg.

'No, please, don't.' Leo whimpered in pain. 'It's down that way,' he pointed down the tunnel.

'That wasn't so hard now was it? Come on John, we have a day to save,' said Bienia. She grabbed the lantern and set off in the indicated direction.

'Sorry Leo,' said John as he carefully stepped over the damaged leg. He then hurried after Bienia, leaving an incapacitated Leo cursing them in the gloom.

The lantern being carried by Bienia soon revealed a blockage in the sewer tunnel ahead. It was a stack of wooden barrels all stamped with the crossed hammers of the Hammerfist Clan.

'Gods,' said Bienia.

She swung the lantern around, looking for something. She soon found it. A fuse ran from the barrels back the way they had just come, held up from the wet floor by bent nails hammered into the wall. Putting the lantern down, she pulled out her knife and cut through the fuse.

'There. Now setting this lot off would be suicidal for anyone trying it.'

John was about to say how relieved he was when they heard a cough from behind them. Turning, they saw a member of the city watch pointing a loaded crossbow at John's head.

'Throw your weapons in the shit,' he ordered.

'It's alright, we're the good guys, we've defused it,' said John.

'Do as I say, now.' The man did not seem impressed.

John carefully complied, all too aware of the sharp and pointy death promised if he did not obey. His sword hit the sewage with a splash, sinking to the bottom. Bienia, on the other hand, hesitated.

'You too,' said the man, adjusting his aim towards Bienia.

Bienia briefly considered throwing the knife at the man, but then sense prevailed, and she threw it into the sewage with a splash. Finally, with obvious emotional pain, her sword followed.

'Now,' the man threw a tinderbox at John's feet, 'light the fuse.'

'What?' said John.

'You heard me, light the fuse. Now.'

It was at this point, that realisation dawned. John realised that this was one of the cities watchmen loyal to Simon Denly. Bienia realised she shouldn't have tossed her weapons in the shit.

'Are you mad? There's no time to get away,' said John.

'Not mad, committed to a cause.'

'You're a bloody loony,' said Bienia.

'That's enough from you, now do as I—'

He was interrupted by a glinting metal dagger tip which suddenly protruded from his neck. His eyes went wide with shock, and he pulled the crossbow trigger. Fortunately, his aim was disrupted, and the crossbow quarrel thumped into Bienia's left arm instead of her head. She let out a grunt of pain as the metal plates were pierced by the steel tipped quarrel and it sank into her bicep.

'My turn to save you,' came Julienne's voice from the shadows beyond the fallen man.

She stepped out into the lantern light, dressed in her usual midnight black outfit. 'Looks like I found you just in time.'

'How did you find us?' asked John.

'Luke finally gave the go-ahead to raid the hideout last night. Fortunately, there was interrogation equipment to hand, and we managed to get the location of the barrels this morning. I came ahead, Rychards men will be here any minute.'

'Did you get Denly?' asked Bienia.

'No, he was long gone. His torturer was still there though,' said Julienne. John thought he detected a note of satisfaction in her voice.

At this point, Lord Rychards men arrived, their mail coats glinting in the lantern light.

'Right lads, let's get this lot shifted somewhere safe,' Julienne ordered, and then said to John and Bienia, 'I think Lord Rychard will want to see the two agents who saved the King...'

She stopped when she saw what the pair were doing. They were wading in the sewer flow and rooting about in an attempt to retrieve their weapons.

'Maybe after a bath and change of clothes,' Julienne added.

CHAPTER 15

John walked into the room where he had previously met Lord Rychard smelling much better than he had a couple of hours ago. His hair was still damp from being washed, and he wore a clean linen shirt and trousers. A stout new pair of boots were on his feet, and a new green cloak completed the ensemble. His soiled clothes and leather armour had been taken away to be burnt, and he had been measured for some new armour by Lord Mayhew's armourer.

Bienia was sitting at the long table and looking at the map of Asterland that was still unrolled in the centre of the table. She was also scrubbed clean and dressed in a clean linen shirt and trousers. Her upper left arm had a fresh dressing on it, and her new grey cloak was draped over the back of a chair.

'Hello, Bee.' John pulled out a chair and sat down. 'What happened to your armour?'

'I don't think I'll ever get the stink out. Apparently, the King is going to pay for a new set to be made.'

'I'm getting new armour too, just been measured for it.'

'I had some muscle-bound oaf taking liberties with my inside leg earlier,' she said.

John couldn't help smiling as he imagined how that particular scene had played out.

'No sign of Lord Rychard yet then?' he asked.

'No. Julienne was here earlier. She said he was on his way and to "behave and don't go anywhere".'

This drew a laugh from John. 'Glad to see you're being patient.'

At that point, her patience was rewarded by the arrival of Lord Rychard and his chief spymaster, Luke. John and Bienia stood up as he entered.

'Sit yourselves down,' he said in a loud, cheerful voice. 'Good job you two, glad you're on the payroll.'

'Thank you, my Lord,' said John, feeling proud. Here he was, the common son of a farmer, being told how great he was by a Lord.

'Well, you've earned your pay. Rest up for a bit before your next assignment.'

'Assignment?' Bienia queried.

'Yes, you'll be travelling with the King's entourage when he leaves on his tour of the northern towns. Luke here will fill you in on the details before you leave.'

Luke smiled knowingly and said, 'Something to look forward to.'

Bienia snorted a short laugh.

'Anyway. Well done, keep up the good work,' said Rychard. He shook their hands and then with a final admonition to 'Carry on!' he turned and left.

'I trust you've found your accommodation satisfactory?' asked Luke.

They had been given rooms in the keep. Their

belongings had been moved there from the Spread Eagle Inn which was now closed until the secret passage could be blocked and the building sold to a new owner.

'It's really something, the bed is amazing,' said John.

'It's alright, bit far from the ground,' said Bienia, not sounding half as impressed as John.

'I apologise. I'm afraid our furniture is not built with the dwarvish stature in mind.' Luke actually did sound regretful. 'Perhaps I could see about getting a new bed made to suit you?'

'Not necessary, I'm not afraid of heights.'

Luke laughed. 'As you wish. I'll leave you two heroes of the hour to enjoy your rest.'

As Luke left the room, he nodded greetings to Julienne who was walking in. She was dressed in similar clean linen clothes as John and Bienia, the first time they had seen her in something other than her usual black. She was grinning from ear to ear as she sat down at the table and pulled a green glass bottle and three pewter goblets out of her leather bag, placing them on top of the map in the middle of the table.

'I think we deserve a celebratory drink,' she said pouring a deep red liquid into the goblets.

'Now you're talking,' said Bienia.

'Please, take the time to savour this. It's from the vineyards of the Sunset Isles and rather expensive.' Julienne finished pouring, raised her glass and said, 'Here's to the best agent team in the kingdom.'

John picked up his goblet and took a sniff, not detecting the slightly vinegary smell he got from wine he could afford, but a decidedly pleasant fruity smell instead. He took a sip, it tasted fantastic too.

Bienia, on the other hand, knocked back the goblet of wine in one go, wiped the back of her hand across her mouth and said, 'Not bad.'

Julienne, having sipped her wine, laughed and said, 'Don't ever change Bienia.'

'Are you coming with us? With the King I mean,' said John.

'Of course. My cover has been well and truly blown around these parts anyway. I'm not a very secret agent with pictures of me distributed far and wide.'

John smiled at that, he still found Julienne fascinating. He knew she was ruthless when she needed to be, but there was something about her. Then there was Bienia, he looked at the dwarven shieldmaiden who was helping herself to more wine. They'd become firm friends over the past few weeks, he knew he could rely on her in a tight situation.

'Is there any food in this keep?' asked Bienia as she lifted her freshly filled goblet. 'And we may need more wine.'

'Well, there's this,' – Julienne pulled a wheel of cheese from her bag – 'and this.' A bulging wine skin followed the cheese onto the table. 'Not as good as the Sunset wine, but hey.' She shrugged.

'Julienne, you are probably the best boss I have ever worked for. Not an arse at all,' said Bienia.

'I second that. So glad we didn't kill you,' said John, a cheeky grin on his face.

'Me too,' said Julienne. 'Now, shall we get on with some serious drinking?'

Thank you for reading **Fire in the North**. On the next few pages you will find the beginning of the next book in the series: **Clans of the Silver Hills**.

CHAPTER 1

King Stephen of Asterland had been residing in the northern border town of Stonebridge for barely two days when the news of an impending attack came. Farmers and their families, carts loaded with their belongings, started arriving in town, looking for safe refuge. They brought news that a dwarven army was heading south. King Stephen immediately ordered scouts to be dispatched to determine the disposition of the force while his men prepared for a fight.

The scouts returned with grim news. There was an army of clan dwarves on the march, and they vastly outnumbered the King's force of just under two hundred men. A war council was called in the watch house, which had been commandeered for the purpose.

'I'm sure you all know the news by now. An invading army of dwarves is heading our way, and their vanguard will likely be here before the day is out.'

The speaker was tall and broad chested, had short brown hair and a neatly trimmed beard. He wore a gleaming suit of chain mail and a simple gold circlet on his head.

This was King Stephen. He was addressing a group of his men-at-arms along with Lords Mayhew and Rychard.

Standing to one side of the room was a short, stocky woman with cropped dark hair. Her name was Bienia Ironfist, and she was keeping quiet. As well as being an agent of King Stephen she was also a dwarf and worried that she would be called on to fight against her clan. She had been asked to attend by Lord Rychard, who ran the King's spy network which she had recently become a part of.

She fidgeted in her new scale armour. It was a good fit but still needed wearing in a bit to feel truly comfortable.

'We need to retreat west to Port Denly,' said Lord Rychard.

'I'll not surrender a square yard of Asterland; we fight them here,' said King Stephen.

Lord Mayhew, the King's cousin and the new Lord of Port Denly, nodded. 'We have the advantage of defending. They must come at us, and they have no cavalry.'

'Yes, our cavalry is an advantage,' said Lord Rychard. 'They are, however, only forty strong. We may be able to defeat their vanguard, but I hate to say it, when the main force gets here we don't stand a chance.'

'Then we'll defeat the vanguard. Give them a bloody nose and then fall back to Port Denly,' said the King.

'In that case, there's someone here who may be able to help,' said Lord Rychard. 'One of your agents travelling with us is a dwarf who has fought in the clan's wars with the goblins.'

Bienia looked around. Yes, she was the only dwarf. He was talking about her. Lord Rychard beckoned her to come forward.

'My lord,' she said, not sure what else she should say.

'What can you tell us of the clan's army?' asked Lord Rychard.

She considered what she knew about her people. 'It's unusual. The clans don't normally come together for a fight unless it's against each other.'

Lord Rychard nodded encouragingly.

'So, don't expect one bit of the army to know what the other is doing. Whoever is in overall command will have their work cut out for them.'

'Well, man, is their vanguard more than one clan?' Lord Rychard directed this question at the man-at-arms who had led the scouting party.

'Don't think so. Only one banner I could see. Crossed hammers.'

'That's the Hammerfist clan,' said Bienia. She was relieved that the Ironfist clan, her clan, were not in the vanguard. 'They're one of the largest. The current High King is Hammerfist. How many are there?'

'Around two to three hundred, all on foot.'

'Dwarves don't do cavalry,' said Bienia. 'Did they have any cannon with them?'

The man-at-arms looked blankly at her.

'Big metal tube things.'

'Didn't see any of those in the vanguard. Just lots and lots of dwarven warriors.'

'That's good news. They're probably all with the main force.'

'Sorry, we didn't get close enough to see.'

Bienia chuckled. 'Fair enough. Today, we only have to worry about crossbows and infantry. They'll fire at you for a bit before getting bored; then they'll come at you in a shield wall.'

'Their vanguard has the advantage of numbers. Any suggestions of how to beat them?' asked King Stephen.

'If you can get behind them with your horses, you can cause havoc. We don't like fighting horsemen, especially if they're the wrong side of the shield wall.'

'There are some trees to the west of the approach we can hide in, then charge 'em from the rear once they're fighting our infantry,' suggested Lord Rychard.

'That should work.' Bienia nodded. 'The clans aren't used to much subtlety in battle. We're used to fighting goblins, and goblins are pretty dumb.'

'Then we have a battle plan,' said King Stephen. He turned to Bienia and said, 'Thank you...' He paused, waiting for her to supply her name.

'Bienia Ironfist, your kingship,' said Bienia.

King Stephen smiled at this unorthodox form of address. 'Thank you, Bienia Ironfist.'

'So, what's it to be, Stephen?' asked Lord Rychard.

'Continue to prepare defences; get the cavalry hidden in those trees. We will fight and defeat the vanguard, then march to Port Denly before the rest of them arrive.'

ABOUT THE AUTHOR

Before realising he'd rather write books instead of code, Richard spent twenty years working as a software engineer. During this time Richard also indulged in socialising through tabletop roleplaying; often as the Gamesmaster and often with a pint of ale! From this was born his passion for, and enjoyment of, storytelling. Richard now spends his days writing and visiting various locations during this pursuit. Officially the local library and, unofficially, the local pub.

Printed in Great Britain
by Amazon